# MAIL ORDER FARMER

## THE WALKER FIVE, BOOK 5

## MARIE JOHNSTON

LE PUBLISHING

Mail Order Farmer

**Destined to be a bachelor...**

As Aaron Walker watched his cousins settle down, he expected to meet that special someone, get married, and maybe even start a family. But women tend to run once the "I live with my parents" revelation comes out. Technically, his parents and brothers live with *him*, but no one seems to be interested in the finer details. The answer? Online dating.

**Resisting her family's well-meaning interference...**

After her dad's death and the loss of his income, Dalisay Cortez dropped out of nursing school. She and her mother live in Manila, struggling to make ends meet, one unexpected bill away from being forced to move in with overbearing relatives. Goodbye city life, and goodbye personal space.

**But what if there was a way out...**

To save them both from an isolated life on the family farm, Dalisay logs onto an international dating site in search of an American husband. Falling in love online is one thing, but leaving everything she knows—including her mom—is harder than Dalisay imagined. What happens when Aaron's idyllic farm life is just like the one she was running from?

For all the latest news, sneak peeks, quarterly short stories, and free material sign up for my newsletter.

*To my aunt Sue. I had a lot of questions when writing this story, and I wish you were still around to ask.*

# CHAPTER 1

*A*aron Walker laughed with his buddy, but it was all an act. Inside, the conversation was hitting too close to home and irritating a sore spot he'd been nurturing for years.

"I mean"—his longtime friend Lucas laughed—"Brock got married before you. I didn't think any girl could get through his thick head."

Aaron bristled but covered his reaction by taking another swig of his Coors. He drained the bottle, the last gulp piss warm.

His cousin Brock's head wasn't thick; he had Autism Spectrum Disorder. He'd found the perfect strong, independent woman. The wedding hadn't been anything more than a sudden phone call and a courthouse visit, but the two weddings before that had involved the entire family, followed by the town. Then a fourth cousin's wedding had been almost as large, with just as much celebration.

That left Aaron odd man out of the Walker Five farm and ranch. One lonely Walker left single while the other four enjoyed wedded bliss. Not that it bothered Aaron at all.

He changed the subject. "How 'bout the Moore Mudders? They had a killer season."

Lucas looked at him with bleary eyes. "I don't follow high school football anymore. When I walked off the field senior year, I was done." He took another sip of his Morgan and Coke. Ice tinkled, and he made a slurping sound.

Aaron rubbed his face. How long had they been at Barley 'n' Hops? Long enough for Lucas to see sloppy drunk in the near future. Aaron eyed his empty bottle and calculated how much longer he'd have to sit before he was good to drive. Technically, he could drive home and be fine, but he hated to flirt with disaster.

The long to-do list he carted around every day wouldn't get done if he was either parked in jail or thumbing it on the highway because he'd lost his license.

Lucas shook his glass at the server walking by. She sauntered over and picked up their empties.

"When'd you get off, Trina?" Lucas asked.

Trina glanced at Aaron. He shrugged in a *what're ya gonna do* way to cover his rampant disappointment. She focused back on Lucas. "I'm going home alone, and you're going back home to your wife."

Lucas's gaze averted. "I was just askin'. Why don't you get me that drink?"

Trina left with more attitude swaying her hips. Lucas looked around, his gaze hitting on every woman, single or not.

"Dude," Aaron said. "I hope you're nothing more than big talk."

"Fuck off." Lucas glowered at the wet ring left on the table. "At least I have someone."

"You won't if you keep doing that."

"Then what's your excuse, Walker? You're like a girl repellent."

"I get plenty of action." His words were empty. Girls ran faster from him than a metal pole in a lightning storm, and he and Lucas always laughed about it. Tonight, it didn't feel so humorous.

Yeah, they thought it was all sweet that he took care of his little brothers. Now that they were not-so-little, the ladies didn't think it was as charming. That's if the subject of him having siblings came up. After a couple of times hitting it at a girl's place, Aaron had to reveal that his parents lived with him. It didn't matter that he didn't live with them but had bought and paid for the house he'd grown up in after his parents moved out. They'd moved back in, and he was the farmer who lived with his parents.

He was starting to doubt he could ever find a woman who'd accept his life situation. He took care of his family. It was what he did. He didn't want a wife who'd abandon them, but damn. They never stuck around long enough to see if he was worth more than a quick fuck.

Lucas hunched over the table. "The only action you get is the ass wiggle as they walk away. I told you that you shouldn't have let Mommy and Daddy move back."

Aaron scowled at his friend. He'd ask when Lucas had grown so negative, but the guy had had too much to drink. He got obstinate and argumentative after a few hours of drinking. Aaron was already prepping himself to wrestle Lucas into his truck to drive him home.

"But I did let them," Aaron said and nodded at Trina as she dropped off the drinks and left.

She was cute. They'd had a thing not too long ago. He'd show up when she was done with work and they'd go back to her place. She had a three-year-old and didn't want to bring men around she wasn't serious with, so he went inside after the sitter left and was gone by dawn. In the light of day, they were nothing more than acquaintances.

Was she still single?

Lucas dove into his drink. Aaron tried to make small talk that didn't revolve around his lack of companionship and Lucas propositioning other women.

His friend slumped to the side, the unfocused gaze on another woman. "Look, Elizabeth What-the-fuck's-her-last-name is in town. Lemme go talk to her."

He veered out of his seat. Aaron scrambled up and blocked him, steadying his drunk friend at the same time.

"Luke, seriously. It's time to go home."

"Fuck you, I'm talking to her." Lucas pushed to go around. Even though he was evenly matched in size to Aaron, he barely budged him. He must be really drunk, or only making a half-hearted effort, like he didn't want to hit on a woman other than his wife.

Why do it then?

"Nope." Aaron tucked him under one arm and grabbed his wallet with the other. He threw some money on the table. They were probably paid up, but stiffing a single mom wasn't an option so he'd rather overpay. "I'm gonna take you home. I've got a long weekend of moving cattle with Cash."

Lucas struggled, more out of pride than putting any real effort into it. "I can drive myself."

"I know. But I'll drive you. You've made it clear all night that I've got nothing better to do."

Lucas snorted and wove out of the bar. The cool late summer air hinted at the weather change they were going to see within a month. Thus his grand plans of harvesting all weekend, then all week, then put on repeat until the crops were in.

He muscled Lucas into his pickup. The height of his Dodge Ram was almost too much, and it was like stuffing a two-hundred-pound sack of unruly potatoes into the passenger seat.

"There you go." He leaned in and buckled Lucas, who glowered out the windshield.

"I can drive myself."

"I know you can," Aaron repeated.

This scenario had become the standard between them the last few months. They went from being inseparable in high school, to drinking and study buddies in college, to Lucas meeting his wife Shaylee and ghosting Aaron. But Aaron had been happy for him, just like he'd been happy watching all his cousins settle down, assuming he'd be in the lineup.

No luck.

Instead Lucas came back around, and it was like they both regressed back to their early days of drinking in bars and trying to find love if only for a night. Lucas had never been someone Aaron thought would cheat, and he didn't think the guy had yet, but he couldn't keep standing by like he supported the efforts.

Aaron got behind the wheel and headed toward Lucas's place. He farmed outside of Moore, on the opposite side of town as Aaron and his family. But where Aaron ran a farm and ranch business with four of his cousins, Lucas was a party of one.

All the lights were off at Lucas's place, not even the exterior house light was on.

"Is Shaylee gone for the weekend?"

Lucas tried for the door handle. It slipped out of his fingers. He refocused, using his whole body, and tried again. Aaron jumped out and ran around before Lucas face planted from the height of the pickup.

He caught Lucas as he slipped out of his seat. That last drink must be hitting him hard.

Slinging Lucas's arm around his shoulders, he steered him toward the door.

Lucas sniffled.

"Don't wipe your nose on me." Aaron glanced over and did a double take. "Are you crying?"

They'd known each other since middle school when they'd both gone out for football. Living on opposite ends of town, they'd gone to different elementary schools. Years of football, baseball, classes, farm injuries, stupid kid injuries… They'd been through it all together. Aaron had been Lucas's best man. In all that time, he'd never seen Lucas cry.

"No." Lucas stared at the dark house.

Just that sloppy drunk. Aaron picked his steps carefully, the lone yard light not reaching the front steps enough to cast more than shadows.

"She left me," Lucas mumbled.

"What?" Aaron said, not paying attention, intent on the rocky path to the door.

"Shaylee. She packed a bag and left. She's in town, shacking up with the dentist."

Shaylee was a dental hygienist. The dentist she worked for was a newly divorced bachelor who had half the single women in town flocking to be his clients. Was that what Aaron needed? A lab coat and glasses that made his eyes look weird?

Thinking of himself at a time like this didn't help Lucas, or him. No wonder Lucas hadn't been acting like himself.

"I'm sorry, man. Wish you would've told me sooner." Aaron could probably pinpoint when Shaylee left based off Lucas's change in behavior. He kicked himself for not digging into it more, but Lucas was a proud farmer. He reached out for help the only way he knew how. Getting drunk and bullshitting.

The dentist was drilling more than teeth while Lucas was getting rebuffed over and over again, adding more drinks to dull the pain.

Once Aaron bumped inside the never-locked door, Lucas shoved away from him. "I can walk on my own."

He shuffled to the leather recliner and slumped into it. His cap popped off his head and he tossed it on the worn carpet next to him.

Aaron glanced around. A basket of laundry sat in the living room and clothing hung inside out off the back of other chairs in the room. He swayed back to peek into the closed off the kitchen. Dirty dishes lined the chipped laminate counter and the square table.

Shaylee had done a lot of the housework because Lucas could be in the field for ten or more hours a day, but this mess wasn't like Lucas. In college, they'd been roommates and he'd been almost fastidious. It was the only time in Aaron's life he hadn't had to pick up after anyone.

Lucas reclined with his head on the headrest, his arms draped over the sides, eyes closed.

"So what happened?" Aaron couldn't leave. He'd definitely have to wait for the worst of the alcohol to flow through Lucas's bloodstream, but his best friend needed a best friend.

"Working all the time. Not giving her enough attention. Don't appreciate what she does around here." Lucas rubbed his eyes and dropped his hand, eyes still shut like it was easier to talk when he didn't see that someone was there listening. "Like...I work long fucking days, man. I'm tired when I come home, but I thought we had a good sex life."

Aaron crossed to the couch and collapsed on it. "But she knew the life when she married you. I mean, she went to school with us."

"Yeah, but she was a city kid, and younger than us, so all she saw was the big, flashy truck." He blinked his eyes open. The room was still dark. Aaron hadn't had time to turn on the lights before Lucas dropped his personal shocker. It was probably better that way. "It's like they don't know that we really use those trucks. For work. Hard work. She gave away the chickens last year, did I tell you?"

Aaron shook his head. There'd probably been a lot of signs Lucas had missed. His happy go-lucky friend had landed hard in reality.

"Yeah. Said she wasn't cut out to butcher the birds. Then I put the kibosh on her idea of an island vacation. Where the fuck would we get the money for it? She said she'd work more. And she did, she must've really worked for it. Well, she won't have to anymore because Dr. Do-me will foot the bill." Bitterness dripped off his last statement.

Aaron stared at his boots. His pant legs were half untucked and, dammit, his boots didn't even match. Luckily both pairs resembled each other enough that maybe it hadn't been obvious in the bar. He should've noticed his haphazard appearance, but he'd thrown food on the table for Jackson and Nicolas after their basketball practice and found something for his aimless dad to do so he'd stay out of Mom's hair. Otherwise those two would bicker incessantly and that wasn't good for the boys to see.

The wedding ring on Lucas's finger was visible only as a darker shadow on his limp hand. Aaron debated whether to ask the next question, but he had to keep the guy talking. "Are you guys going to get a divorce?"

Lucas glared at the far wall where his wedding picture hung. The happy bride smiled serenely next to Lucas as she lifted one side of her dress to reveal a cowboy boot; shoes Lucas never wore. Another early sign Shaylee thought she was marrying something she wasn't: the sexy cowboy with money flying out of his wallet and his finger in all the city council business.

Nope. They were farmers. Aaron's own operation achieved financial success because his dad and his uncles had combined all their land and formed the Walker Five. Aaron and the rest of the new five grew up learning the ins and outs and educated themselves. The ranch supplemented the farm if it was a bad growing season, but they could still weather a few bad years without the cattle income.

"D-i-v-o-r-c-e," Lucas said morosely. "She hasn't filed, yet, but I will. If she thought this was some cry for help, she could've done it without hooking up with someone else. No, I'm done. I give you shit that no one's going to tolerate your hot mess of a family life, dude, but the reality is you're the lucky one. That way you don't get roped into the lie that is marriage. You don't get saddled with the woman who wants you to make all the money and shower her with it, then bitch about all the hours you put in to do it. We ain't going to find anything real with our work, and that's the truth."

"But our parents—"

"Different time, man." Lucas fell quiet, then snorted. "Your parents should've gotten divorced ages ago. I don't think I went to your house once when they weren't arguing."

"They don't argue, they needle each other. They feed off it." Aaron should've grown up to expect the same dynamics in his own relationships, but he'd been surrounded by solid marriages. All his aunts and uncles were still married, except for Dillon's mom, who was widowed.

Lucas sighed, and his lids drifted shut. "Face it, dude. We're decent guys and that's not what women want. This life, us, it's not what they dream of."

Aaron waited a few minutes without saying anything. Lucas's breathing steadied. He was asleep. Aaron glanced at the clock ticking above the bookshelf. Eleven. He should be climbing into bed, enjoying the warmth before he had to get up and work in the chilled air all day.

*It's not what women really want.*

Hope had bloomed eternal since Aaron had gone on his first date. But now he was twenty-nine. Was he destined to be Uncle Aaron, the bachelor uncle who dressed funny and cracked stupid jokes everyone rolled their eyes at?

Well, he didn't crack jokes, so there was that.

Lucas snoozed, but Aaron wasn't comfortable leaving. He puttered around the house, snagging laundry and tossing it into a pile for washing. No matter how good a friend Lucas was, Aaron wasn't sniff testing the man's laundry.

In the kitchen, he stacked dishes and emptied the dishwasher. Ten minutes had passed. With a heavy sigh, he filled the dishwasher, started it, and hand washed the rest. The floor needed a good sweep, and it got it.

Another glance at his friend. Hell, he'd been around Lucas much more drunk than this. It was probably all right to go. He slid off the man's work boots and covered him with a blanket before going back out to his truck.

The cab was still warm, and Aaron sat behind the wheel staring at the dark yard. His house wasn't much different than the one in front of him. His dad was the oldest and had built their house before the other uncles. It was a 1980s sprawling ranch with two bedrooms and an office upstairs and three downstairs bedrooms with a moderately sized family room.

Growing up, it'd been enough room for his parents, Aaron, and his brothers. These days, it could feel claustrophobic with his brothers fighting the way teenage boys do and his parents carrying on the way they did.

What a pleasant thought. At least everyone might be asleep by the time he got back. One of the few moments he got to himself.

He drove home. The streets were quiet and once he left city limits, he didn't come across another car. Heading down the road to his house, he passed the first of his cousins' places. Cash's house was on his right, the trees failing to conceal the barns and corrals. Dillon was on the left, his trees fully enclosing his property, only the soft glow of a yard light lifted over the tops.

Brock's was the next on his left. The trees blocked his house, but Aaron knew there'd be no lights on other than the yard and outside house light. Brock hit his bedtime like clockwork, especially now that he had Josie and didn't have to make excuses for why it was so important to him to get to bed after the nightly news.

He reached the dead-end that his house was on. To the right would be Travis's place where he was probably snuggled in bed next to Kami after reading the latest issue of *The Progressive Farmer*.

And there was his property. Half the lights were on even though his family were probably each in their bedrooms. His brothers' beater trucks sat askance in the driveway, blocking the garage where his mom kept her car. Aaron idled to the big rectangular shop a hundred yards from his house and parked in front of it. He killed the engine and crossed to his home, his boots crunching on the gravel the only sound in the night.

The warm glow of alcohol had faded long before driving Lucas home. He shivered and shoved his hands into his pockets. Lifting his gaze to the sky, he slowed to take in the myriad of stars above him. The Big Dipper, his favorite, dominated with its three handle stars the brightest in the sky. Nights like this, he could tolerate stargazing. In another month, especially when January descended, the long walk across the yard from the only decent place to park his truck would be too frigid to linger long, but that was when the stars were the most brilliant.

Letting himself into the house, he eased the screen door shut. Quietly, he toed off his boots and shut off lights as he made his way to the master bedroom at the end of the house. His parents hadn't insisted on getting their original room back. The arrangement was supposed to only have been for a few months, but three years later…

They stayed downstairs in his old bedroom and his brothers had moved into the other two bedrooms down there.

No one bothered Aaron and there was no noise coming from anywhere in the house. On the way, he stepped into the tiny office and grabbed his laptop from the cluttered desk. Ledgers threatened to spill to the floor, but he shoved them back with the edge of the computer and backed out.

A subdued energy swirled inside his gut. Changing into a T-shirt and shorts, he glanced at the computer. He should go to bed.

Sliding under the covers, he rolled them down and pulled the laptop close. It fired right up because he'd used it to balance accounts for the fall season before Lucas had called.

Without thinking too hard, he typed "Tinder" into the search bar. A few minutes of searching showed it wasn't what he was looking for. Women from places like L.A., Orlando, or hell, even Minneapolis in his home state of Minnesota weren't likely to prefer life in rural solitude. Would he invest all that time in the "getting to know" stage only to find out they weren't in it for more than a good time?

What about long-term? A real relationship?

He shoved his hands through his hair.

What the hell was he thinking? Dating sites?

But didn't old man Farley marry a lady he…uh, ordered? Aaron tried to remember the gossip. It'd been several years, but yes, the woman had been from Russia.

Weren't they still married?

But were they happy? Mr. Farley might be, but was she?

No, this was stupid. Aaron shut the lid of the computer and stared at the wall. Shelves in the corner held various hats that he wore. The closet door was half open and his pants were spilling out. He'd have to ask his parents to help him catch up on laundry.

He was almost thirty and he'd have to ask his parents, who still lived with him, to help with laundry.

What lady was going to take the time to get to know him?

The screen was back up and lit. For an hour, he cruised various online dating sites, bypassing the uber sexy photos. He'd linger over the attractive headshots and wonder if the woman existed or if either the photo or information was fake.

This was pointless. If he could spark an online relationship, who was going to move to the middle of the country, to the middle of nowhere?

Where had Farley's bride been from?

Was she happy? Were they happy?

He punched in "mail order" and his hand stayed over the "b" for bride. God, he couldn't do it.

The lid was half closed again, when he paused. The quiet house with all the lights on and no place to park. Trina saying he came with more baggage than she did. Lucas passed out and brokenhearted in his empty home.

He flipped it open and entered "international brides." What pulled up sank his stomach faster than a hunk of lead in a pool. He couldn't, just couldn't, do mail order. A man had his pride, and yes, he was lonely and scared to be a bachelor for life, but rather that than a miserable woman who felt she had no other options.

He deleted the search and entered "international dating." A page full of dating sites from a mix of countries popped up.

What would it hurt just to take a look?

# CHAPTER 2

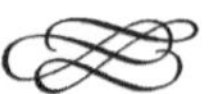

Dalisay Calamba Cortez skirted into her home and dragged in a deep breath. Her heart was pounding, and she found little comfort in the familiar noise of the street filtering into the apartment she shared with her mother. Navigating the streets of Manila at midnight was a different beast than in the middle of the day. She'd barely evaded a group of swaggering young men that spelled nothing but trouble for a lone woman.

"Dali, is that you?"

"It's me, Ina. I'm home." She set the bag that held her phone and wallet on the rickety end table by the door and threw the deadbolt.

The slithery sensation that plagued her on every walk home danced along her spine. She shivered. The small lamp flickering on the end table was as good as a lighthouse, signaling that there may be danger in the area, but there was also a shore offering safety.

Her mom came out, her robe tucked tight around her petite body and her straight black hair tucked into a bun. Dalisay had hit five feet and maxed out, but that was still a few inches taller than her mom. Despite her height, Mari Cortez, her dear Ina, had the swagger of a six-foot-tall man.

Ina blinked into the kitchen light. "You shouldn't be working so late."

Dalisay agreed. "I was promised a raise if I took the evening shift manager position." She should've worked the overnight shift. It'd be safer treading home in the morning with the early work traffic.

Ina clicked her tongue, her expression grim. "If your father found out you were on the streets by yourself close to midnight..."

Sadness tugged at Dalisay's heart. Four years since his work accident on the bumpy provincial roads and the pain was finally lessening, or she was just used to it. Yes, he would've been indignant that she was putting herself at risk.

But he was gone, and so was his income stream. Their lower middle-class standard was dropping. She and Ina would have to move out of this apartment, which was in a fairly decent part of the city. An outcome she didn't desire, and she suspected her mother wanted to stay in Manila as much as she did.

"It's more money." Dalisay cast a longing look toward her room, exhausted from a long shift. Her job at the internet café was as enjoyable as it could be. Customers were more concerned with what was on their screen than in her. Her coworkers were pleasing enough, although some nights were more difficult than others to listen to their optimistic outlooks of the future. But it was a decent job, since she couldn't attend university as planned after her dad's passing.

"Money isn't everything. Your safety is more important."

"I know, Ina." Dalisay's words rang hollow. But unless Ina planned to remarry—and since Dalisay had heard her muttering as if her father were in the room, she wasn't—or Dalisay said her vows soon, their options were few.

She got hit on a lot at work. Having worked at the café since her dad's death four years ago, she knew some of the regulars. Knew they were married or seeing someone. Knew that as they propositioned her, checking out her legs in her short black skirt, peeking through her transparent white blouse for a glimpse of cleavage, or more. It came with the job. Unfortunately, no serious romantic prospects came with the position.

She'd almost walked down the aisle two years ago when she was twenty-one. Until her cheating fiancé had showed his true colors.

*I'll pay her as a mistress. You won't even know she's around.*

Uh-huh. The disgusting thought of sharing her man made her a little rage-y. She might be from the province, but she still expected her spouse to be monogamous. She'd flown out of primary school, fleeing an isolated life under her loving father's gentle but firm rule, and hit Manila exactly like every other girl her age moving to the encompassing city from the rural areas of the Philippines.

The freedom had been exhilarating, though the smog had been stifling, the traffic loud, and it took a solid year to fall asleep to the constant horn honking resonating from the streets. Her father had worried, but she'd studied hard and his pride at her grades fueled his glow. Then he was gone.

Her mother's family had swooped in to help, urged Dalisay to come back home as they cared for Ina in her grief. Her uncle, Peejong, had seamlessly filled the authority role her father had left.

Dalisay's refusals had sounded weak compared to Peejong's ill-disguised pleas to return home and help her mother. He worried about her in the city, was concerned about their finances, but by then Dalisay had met her ex.

Hindsight meant it was now clear how much she'd rushed things with her ex in an effort to stay at university. The warning signs that he couldn't commit to, well, anything, had run rampant and she'd deliberately ignored them, convincing herself it was the grief and stress inciting her paranoia.

She'd steeled herself to stand up to her mother during their next phone call, when Ina had packed a bag, announced she couldn't be haunted by her husband's death, and moved to Manila to live with Dalisay.

The appearance of Ina had been as sudden as the loss her father, but not as disruptive. Apparently, Dalisay wasn't the only female in her family looking for what else life had to offer.

Ina arriving loaded with two suitcases, and her smile only highlighted how much Dalisay had missed her family. That didn't mean she wanted to move back to the province, though. Maybe someday, but not while she was young and single.

Nights like tonight when Dalisay could come home to a comforting face after a harrowing commute made her ponder how long she would've held out against Peejong without Ina.

"Good night." Dalisay kissed the top of Ina's head and headed to her room.

"Peejong called tonight." Ina's grave tone stopped Dalisay in her tracks.

Dalisay turned around. "Is everything okay?"

Ina rubbed her eyes. "He wants us both to move back."

A beat of homesickness hit her. She missed her extended family and their farm in the middle of lush greenery. The rise of mountains, the clear air, and silent nights beckoned her, but where she was from, there was also a lack of jobs, fewer professional opportunities, and more family who thought they had a say in her future. Growing up amid all her kin provided a grounding experience, something she both missed and worked hard not to go back to. After nearly five years in the city on her own, it was also something she couldn't readily go back to. Not without an anchor for herself so she didn't get swept along with what others thought was best.

Ina folded her arms, her expression troubled. "He said he talked to Michael today. You remember their neighbor boy a couple of years older than you?"

Dalisay pursed her lips, knowing exactly where this was going.

"Peejong gushed about Michael's accomplishments. He's a mechanic; owns his own garage in Solano." Ina shot her a pointed look. "And he's single."

"Did Peejong find all that out, or was it Sally?" If Peejong was a gale force wind, her aunt Sally was a hurricane. Except hurricanes were chaotic, leaving behind devastation. Aunt Sally was the steady wind that wore away centuries of granite, smoothing the surface to its preferences.

Peejong was Ina's older brother. Therefore, Sally assumed responsibility for all his younger siblings. Ina never let on how much it bothered her, but her moving in was enough evidence.

Ina didn't reply, but as was the way with her mother, what she didn't say was filled to the brim with information.

Dalisay shook her head. "And I suppose Michael still lives around Solano?" He'd been a nice enough young man, but there'd been zero chemistry between them, and she didn't want an empty marriage. Or a relationship strongly influenced by outside sources.

She wanted a union where she and her husband formed a strong wall against the outside world.

Ina didn't say anything. The lamplight cast shadows across half of her face, deepening the worry lines at the corner of her eyes. Honks and bleats from Jeepneys filtered in through the thin glass windows. The cloying heat didn't decrease much at night, but Ina had shut off the tiny air conditioning unit.

"The money is running out, Dali. In less than a year, we either move to the slums, or back to the province."

The slums. Where shanties couldn't keep out typhoon rain and winds and flooding was a constant problem. They could lose their home to a gust of wind and their belongings to anyone with more muscle than them. A giant loss of physical and mental security.

And if she moved back, she'd be beholden to Peejong and Sally and probably lonely enough to marry Nice Enough Michael. Ina would feel relegated to a burden, and her pride wouldn't withstand that.

Then Sally would start on about how babies made the solitude easier. She had slipped in a few comments here and there when Dalisay had been engaged.

Yes, Dalisay wanted kids. Not necessarily with Michael. And what if Michael was seeing someone, or lacked as much interest as she did?

She'd lost her dad. She'd lost her dream of becoming a nurse. Now both she and Ina were facing the loss of their independence. Of something as simple as sleeping in separate rooms because the house at the farm wasn't large enough for all of them. "The internet."

Dalisay's mouth snapped shut. Was she really going to suggest what came to mind?

No. Ina would never go for it.

"Yes?" Ina stared at her, as if sensing Dalisay might be forming a plan.

They couldn't afford the internet on their income, but it was a bonus of working at the internet café. She had access off hours, and Ina got a discount for her own job hunt when she wasn't selling at the market. It was how she could carry out the crazy idea that was forming.

"I can find a husband on the internet. An American. I'll go there where you won't have to worry about getting through the city at night."

"But… Find a man online?" Ina shook her head. "Is that what you want?"

Dalisay had one friend in university who'd run off with an expat. She lived in a village Dalisay couldn't afford to visit. How was she doing? The man had been considerably older, but that didn't make as much a difference in how he'd treated her friend. The last time Dalisay talked to her, she'd been happy, disgustingly so because Dalisay had just found out her ex had another girlfriend—but that had been before her broken-off wedding.

But what about leaving Ina? "What I don't want is to work for Peejong and Sally the rest of my life. And you'd be free to find the housekeeping job you talked about."

Ina hadn't applied for any live-in housekeeping jobs because Dalisay couldn't make the rent without her.

Ina glanced away. She was seriously considering it. Dalisay worried her lower lip. Find an American husband? But Ina would be free to find a job that'd give her a roof over her head, and Dalisay would look for a partner she could fall in love with someday.

She continued making her case. "Maybe I could go somewhere I could finish my degree." Her heart jumped at the thought of getting her dream back, of being able to finally finish nursing school.

Could she do it? Marry a stranger? Be happy like her friend?

"I don't know about this." Her mom crossed to her and set her hands on her shoulders. "But I do know that I can't stay up waiting and having small heart attacks every minute you're late. And I can't be the reason you go back home to be miserable. And I know you loved university."

A beat of doubt went through her. If Ina was on board, this was more than a crazy plan. "And I can send money home."

How would she know where to start? She'd heard about different outcomes than her friend's good fortune. Horror stories whispered in the dark between her and her old friends about someone who knew someone who'd met a guy online and was never heard from again. Or someone who knew someone who knew someone else who'd met a guy online and had become nothing more than his personal sex doll that also cleaned house.

Meeting a decent husband was one thing. Getting sold into slavery was another.

Still, there were hundreds of women just like her who did it every year. But there was no way to know how it turned out for each of them.

Ina shuffled to a chair. Dalisay looked longingly at her room. Her feet were sore, and her adrenaline was waning after her trek home. Rest would have to wait. This was too serious of a topic.

Did the women who married and moved to America live in a place where they feared being out after dark? And were extra cautious during the day?

"I still don't know, Dali."

"I'll be careful."

"We'll be careful. You're not doing this alone."

Dalisay smiled. "We'll research the stories of how it went wrong and learn what to look for. There's a better life out there for us, and we're going to have to pursue it." After a ton of research. Just checking it out didn't mean she'd be married off as soon as she clicked. "If I stay and research, then I can walk home in the morning."

A frown passed through Ina's features. "I don't like you

being up all night, but it might be safer. I'll go on my days off to check on the men interested in you."

This was quite the turning point in her life. Within minutes, she'd gone from jilted bride barely making a living, to woman seeking an American man.

Because, like Ina, she wanted more for herself, and this city had a way of bleeding a person dry as the margin of middle class disappeared, but spooned a person enough freedom and possibility to make them stay.

Moving to America, though? With a man? For a man?

She missed intimacy, and she wanted love, but a stranger?

"Maybe you'll find a guy here," Ina said.

"How, when I'm working all the time? When there's a hundred other girls throwing themselves at him?" Could she find a man she trusted?

Ina sat back with a sigh. "I guess we're doing this, then."

She could do this. For her family, for herself. There had to be a nice man out there to build a life with.

America, then.

# CHAPTER 3

Scowling at the screen, Aaron scrolled through women who'd "bumped" him in the international dating app he'd chosen. Profile pictures ranged from sweet and innocent to holy shit—boobs.

When he'd first started on this adventure a month ago, he'd spent all his nights researching the process. Narrowing his search down to a country seemed his first major move.

How does someone say, *I'm going to marry someone from Russia.* Or *my bride will be from Colombia.* He found pages that generally outlined what to expect from each country's women.

He'd almost abandoned his efforts. This wasn't shopping for tractors and reading reviews from content customers and pinpointing trouble issues. These were people. One sweeping statement didn't represent the entire population.

But he persisted. Because his female friends had already said what they wanted wasn't him.

The reports of family values and strong family dedication of Filipina women drew him to a popular dating site meant to pair Filipinas with American men. He fought off another undercurrent of seediness. Reading through blogs and forums, it really seemed like some women were looking for true love with a decent partner and he hung on to that.

Still, it was one thing to read about a bunch of men saying how faithful and loyal the gorgeous women of the Philippines were, but what did the women have to say? After more than a few hours of searching, he finally deduced that yes, many had built the loving relationship they'd been seeking.

It heartened him.

Until Victoria. He'd bumped her, and she'd responded. They'd started emailing until she'd asked to Skype him after a week of correspondence. He'd been a bundle of nerves that first time, but she'd been sweet and giggly. Something had felt off, like the chemistry wasn't right between them, but since it'd been such a short time, he didn't want to end it.

Then she'd laid out the story of her sick mom and her disabled brother and how badly they needed money for her mom's surgery. So badly that he should wire it as soon as possible.

He'd been torn. Should he just help her even if he knew she was probably scamming him? After more research, he found that some of these scammers could harvest hundreds of thousands of sob-story dollars.

With a heavy heart, he'd cut ties and prayed she hadn't been telling the truth.

Who could he trust now? Would he wade through profiles for years, getting to know a girl before he found out they either didn't gel, or that she was trying to milk him for money? He might as well stay in the dismal dating scene of Moore.

He received notice of a new "bump." Daisy was the name on the account. He clicked on her profile, the thumbnail of her photo barely visible.

Her photo expanded, and his heart thudded. She was…

enticing. Her smile looked genuine, not a put-on for the camera but more like someone had caught her off guard in the middle of a laugh. Her lips were full and a rich pink, but she didn't seem to be wearing lipstick. Unlike a few of the profiles where the women had vamped up, Daisy had chosen a natural look.. Her black hair was long and draped over one shoulder, and dark lashes rimmed around her eyes, giving her natural eyeliner. Was her skin as soft as it looked? As luminous in real life?

She couldn't be real.

He stared at the photo too long before he tore his eyes away to read her summary. She worked at an internet café and was willing to move to America if she met the right person. Her extended family lived in the province, but she lived with her mother in Metro Manila, who had moved in with her after her father had died.

The interests she listed were reading and biking and hanging out with her mother. That was it. No favorite color. Nothing about what she looked for in a guy. Short and to the point, like there was no reason to exert effort beyond that. He could get behind that feeling. Why lay it all out there for some creeper to latch onto and target her with?

He bumped her back. And waited. It was ten p.m. his time. At thirteen hours ahead, it'd be eleven a.m. her time.

He waited some more. There was no desire to look at anyone else. He shut the lid and went to bed.

# CHAPTER 4

Dalisay looked around. It wasn't unusual for workers to jump on after shifts. No one was paying attention to her. At this time of night, there were only a few young men and women at the computer terminals. She logged onto the dating site and stared at the number of men who'd bumped her. Many of them were older. She didn't rule them out, but they didn't interest her. She sifted through men with sunglasses, men with graying hair, men with no hair, and more until a familiar photo stopped her.

*Yes.* He had bumped back.

She chewed on her lower lip. A. W. was the screen name he went by. What did the A stand for? She'd been searching for a month. Her mother had been searching for a month. Ina gravitated to the older crowd, and when Dalisay protested Ina had insisted that they were likely more financially stable and had less stringent ideas of a relationship.

Ina hadn't found A. W., though. The distinct blue of his eyes had stopped Dalisay mid scroll. He lived in Minnesota, and when Dalisay had researched the state, she'd found the scenery was stunning. Green, much like the province, but not as lush and with no mountains. And Minnesota had snow.

It wasn't until she landed on A. W.'s profile that the idea of culture shock had set in. This was the first profile that had made her stop to think about uprooting her life. She'd be removed from everything she knew, even the weather. She'd be alone, except for a new stranger she was supposed to marry. Moving to Manila had overturned her life. Going from a quiet, calm life with only the necessities, to the hustle and bustle and excess of city life. How hard would it be to adjust to another country?

Those were all worries for a different day. She opened A. W.'s message.

"Thanks for the bump, Daisy. My name's Aaron if you want to talk some more."

That was it. Yes, she wanted to talk more. Her fingers shook over the keyboard. This was the most serious she'd gotten about the whole idea. And that was all it had seemed to be as she and Ina researched and set up accounts and screened prospective husbands. Their thoughts had been steeped in thoroughness and protection. Neither she, nor her mother, wanted to fall for the suave lines of a predator.

She inhaled and let it out slowly. Just replying didn't mean she had to marry him. There were still a lot more steps between returning his greeting and meeting him.

Her gaze landed on his profile photo. The sun blazed behind him, his easy grin making his blue eyes twinkle. Those eyes were mesmerizing with their slight squint. What season was this taken in?

She distracted herself and searched what season late October would be in Minnesota.

Almost winter. She shuddered. How warm did their summers get?

Back on his profile, her gaze swept over his coppery hair and his broad shoulders.

He appealed to her, there was no denying it. But was this what A. W.—Aaron—even looked like?

She typed a reply before she could talk herself out of it. The money in savings was draining quickly.

The reminder spurred her response. She didn't have much to tell about herself. Reading through other women's profiles hadn't made sense: I like sunsets, poems, and romantic walks.

Please. The sunset was hard to see through the pollution plaguing Manila. She'd rather help her mom roll lumpia than read a poem, and her idea of a romantic walk was having someone with her that would scare off would-be abductors.

She stuck with the food subject in her reply. Her father used to gush about how her mom's adobo had won his heart. Dalisay had learned how to prepare all the basics, and she and her mother often competed to make the hottest salsa and laughed over how much their fingers burned after chopping the peppers.

A cloud of sadness stalled her fingers. If this Aaron was a decent guy, she'd be moving. Not soon, but eventually, and Ina would stay behind.

Dalisay rubbed her chest. But Ina would be taken care of. A good job, with a roof over her head, and Dalisay would make sure to send money home.

A hot tear rolled down her cheek as she finished up her message. She'd wait to hear more from him before she asked to chat over the internet. Ina was going to buy a webcam to Skype in case they couldn't reserve the computers with the cams, or if they weren't working. Dalisay hated that they had to waste money on that, but her mother had told her to consider it an investment.

She proofread her message. How inane. She liked her

mom's cooking, cooked herself, didn't finish university, and yep, she'd like to talk more.

She hit send.

Dalisay sniffled. Her discounted time was running out. Ina insisted she use some of her earnings to stay in the café until morning. It blew all of the manager raise she'd gotten, but the relief was almost worth it. If she kept walking home at night, she'd either end up in a nightmare or dead.

She should check the other profiles and initiate conversations, but she didn't. The rest of her late night/early morning was spent combing Minnesota facts. She put "Aaron W Minnesota" into the search but nothing useful came out. He might be buried in the results, but it'd only add to her torture of who he was.

Fighting off her eyelid droop was growing impossible when the sky started to lighten. She logged off, fatigue weighing on her like she'd been running and filling orders all through the night. Those long hours might've been a waste of money, but an oddly optimistic sensation followed her home.

She darted through the streets as traffic steadily increased by the minute.

When she came through the door of her apartment, Ina stood, slicing peppers at the counter. "What'd you find?" she asked without missing a beat in her food prep. "I'm making an omelet. Sit and fill me in."

The muscle-numbing weariness Dalisay had been battling all night dulled to a constant battle of keeping her eyes open. She was home with Ina. Two more nights and she'd have a day off.

"I made contact. Tentative."

Her mom nodded, her mouth turned down in concentration. "With how many men?"

"One. There were others, but I wasn't drawn to them."

Ina glanced up, one brow quirked.

Dalisay shrugged, the sense of being interrogated daunting. Ina won that round every time. "This man's name is Aaron and he's younger. Closer to my age."

"Don't trust him."

"I don't either, Ina. Not yet." Something about him, though… No, she had to be careful.

"I tell you, the older ones are financially stable. They have fewer expectations beyond a happy wife, happy life."

"I don't want to write off this guy until I know more."

"Dali, we're running out of time. The older guys are safer."

"But the traffickers know that and maybe those profiles are fake."

Ina paused mid-chop. She nodded and continued dicing the tomato. "You still need to try. Did you bump any of them back?"

Dalisay worried her lower lip. All those hours spent on a state and not a man. "I was looking up Minnesota. It's where Aaron's from."

Ina rolled her eyes up to the ceiling. "Dali." She chopped some more, her mouth in a flat line. Dalisay squirmed in her seat. "Fine. What'd you find about Minnesota? Where is it?"

She couldn't stop her grin. Life in the city had relaxed Ina in many ways. Like she could only take so much stress and had to pick and choose where to put her worries.

Dalisay unloaded all of her Minnesota knowledge as she jumped in to prepare the rice to go with the omelet. Her mother nodded but didn't interrupt.

When Dalisay was done, breakfast was ready. They sat to eat at their small square table. Ina led the prayer and they ate. Moments like this brought back fond memories of attending mass as a family. Since Ina had left Solano, she hadn't found a new church. Another strike against her in Sally's eyes.

The last bite was gone when Dalisay's eyelids refused to stay up any longer. She had to be up soon for her shift. "Ina, I must sleep."

"Go. I'll clean up. But, Dali, I will go with tomorrow to see this Aaron, and after work you will bump more of those older men."

"Yes, Ina."

The few hours of sleep went by too quickly and she was up again and heading back to work. Ina joined her on the bus ride to the café, her tote bag clutched close to her body. In the café, Dalisay trotted back to the kitchen while her mother got settled at a terminal.

Dalisay dropped a tea next to her mother. Ina glanced up in surprise.

"It's on me," Dalisay said. The woman had slept less than she had.

"He's a farmer," Ina said in a whisper.

Dalisay's gaze switched to the screen. Ina had logged in already and had read through the messages. Dalisay's heart jumped at the sight of his smile. Did he have a sense of humor?

A long message was laid out under his photo.

She sucked in a breath and looked around. "Is that from him?" Leaning down, she skimmed his message.

He was a farmer who worked with his family. The foods he grew were listed, along with the menagerie of animals on his farm. Sunflowers, wheat, soybeans, cattle, and sheep.

"Horses?" she squeaked. Oops. She straightened and looked around. New customers were coming in. She'd have to wait to linger over the information he gave.

"He sounds promising, but Dali. A farmer."

"He's not Peejong," Dalisay whispered and went back to work.

She didn't want to get her hopes up, had to stay aware of

the dangers, but if it helped her get through a long shift on a few hours of sleep, then she would let the fantasies flow. Because as she daydreamed about an idyllic life with a handsome farmer, Ina was bumping older men.

AARON UNSADDLED TWITTY, the bay stomping his hooves. Twitty was the best cutting horse he'd ever had for cattle, but he could be stubborn and ornery, like everyone else in Aaron's life. Today, they'd only had to move cattle to the winter pasture, but Twitty had exerted what control he could to cut cattle off from the entrance. The horse wanted out of the elements and back in his pasture. Aaron did, too, but Twitty's behavior didn't speed up the process.

The wind sliced across his face. His complexion was probably as ruddy as his hair after being exposed to the cold all day.

Lucas had called to go out, but Aaron had passed. Drinking wasn't doing Lucas any good and Aaron didn't want to enable him. That was as good of an excuse as any to trade messages with Daisy for the last week. She'd asked to Skype. To chat at a good time for her, he would have to be camera ready by one in the morning. He'd asked about phone calls or apps, but she was limited with her phone's capabilities.

With the other girl, Victoria, she'd Skyped whenever was good for him, but Daisy said she worked in the evenings. He believed her.

Her sweet emails were eye opening. Her words had an innocent but mature quality. No guile had come through the screen, but perhaps he'd get a different sense when they spoke. She'd been honest about a previous engagement that had fallen through due to infidelity. He wished he could be as honest, but "Hey, my parents and two brothers live with me" never made it through. Five times he'd typed it, and five times it'd been deleted.

Let her get to know him first. If it was just her and her mother, it could overwhelm her.

He brushed Twitty down and let him out into the pasture. Nightfall came earlier this time of year and it was already dark. He headed toward the house. The basement lights were on, the flicker of the TV coming from the egress windows. His mom was probably on the computer, combing Pinterest for her next big project that she never started. His dad was probably in the recliner on his second or third beer. Hopefully, they had decided on a program to watch and the arguing would be at a minimum.

Warmth encompassed him as he entered his house. The mudroom dripped with coats. There were no hooks left for his. How the hell had they done it when his brothers were younger before his parents had tried moving them to town? The boots and coats were bigger than in those days.

Jackson was going to college after next summer and would only be home on the weekends, during breaks, and all summer. Nicolas would be a senior.

Aaron draped his coat on the bench and toed his boots off. Something smelled good. He assigned his brothers cooking nights and tonight had been Nicolas's, unless he traded with Jackson because it was Friday and out of all of them, Nicolas had a more active personal life.

Aaron went in search of leftovers. The fridge revealed a small container of beef stroganoff that might feed a toddler.

"Thanks a lot," he muttered.

He dug out bread and lunchmeat and assembled a sandwich. As he was wolfing it down, Nicolas passed through on a wave of cologne.

"Whoa," Aaron said around a mouthful, "ease up on the Axe."

"It'll lighten up. It's fresh."

Not at those quantities. "Whatcha doing tonight?"

Nicolas sighed and turned around. "Emily's parents said I could come over and watch a movie. As long as we leave all the lights on. And we sit in separate chairs."

"That's awful. You gonna be all right?" Aaron grinned at his brother's scowl. He wanted to high-five Emily's parents.

"I wouldn't mind touching my girlfriend."

"Yeah, they know that."

Nicolas snorted. "One of us in the family should be getting some action."

Aaron pushed off the counter. "One, Emily is your girlfriend and you shouldn't talk about her that way. Two, how can I get action? I'm too weak because no one leaves me any fucking dinner."

"Sorry," Nicolas grumbled. "None of us expected it to turn out that good."

"Next time, set some aside in a dish." It really wasn't a big deal, but if their parents weren't going to teach them manners, it was up to Aaron.

So many times he wanted to ask his parents if they'd given up after him. He recalled how strict they'd been about what he watched, what he ate, and saying "please" and "thank you." Then he'd been ten and Jackson had come along, and they had let it all hang out. With Nicolas, it'd gotten even worse. Aaron blazed the trail; his brothers reaped the bennies.

It was why he'd told them to move back in when his parents had flailed on their own. His dad couldn't hold a job, despite getting up at dawn and farming all day since he could walk. Mom hadn't fared much better. She'd held a job but was so miserable, everyone wished they'd fire her.

Dad tinkered on the farm all day and pitched in when they needed an extra set of hands. He was anxiously awaiting Dillon's baby being born in the spring so he could take over that share of the planting. This was supposed to be the guy's golden years.

"I'll make sure Jackson portions some off for you next time." Nicolas's grin held a wicked glint. "He fancies himself the next Pioneer Woman, only he can't cook."

"If he followed the recipe, he'd be fine." But Aaron would eat whatever his brothers cooked because they needed the support. They needed the skills that'd carry them out of the house and into the real world.

If only they'd tackle laundry with as much enthusiasm as cooking.

He saw Nicolas off and went back to his room. There were still hours left before his call to Daisy. Scratching the back of his neck, he looked around for something to work on. It wasn't in his nature to sit still and around his place, there was too much to do.

Part of him burst to tell his cousins, even Lucas, about Daisy. He couldn't yet. They'd see it as nothing more than a desperate attempt to get a wife. Short of showing them the emails that she appeared to be a real woman, he didn't have much rebuttal.

From his research, the most common route to marriage was to chat online, then he'd fly over and meet her in person. If the chemistry proved to be real, and Daisy and her family approved of him, then he'd fly home and apply for a K-1 visa to bring her over.

He could probably get married in the Philippines, but then his family would miss out and he hadn't waded through the legal speak to know if he could bring her home right away. Besides, that really did feel more mail-order bride. He wanted a relationship, one with depth. In reality, he couldn't risk getting stuck in another country.

The Walker Five was expanding and they needed everyone working. Sure, his dad could help, but he wasn't up to working full time anymore. His brothers had lives and colleges to tour, or in Jackson's case, would be moving away entirely. No. Aaron would have to be patient.

That is, if he and Daisy worked as a couple.

A load of laundry, a quick chat with his parents, and emptying the dishwasher brought him to the nightly news.

He sat down to watch and figure out what he'd do from ten thirty to one a.m. The long day of cold air and hard work caught up to him. He relaxed into the chair, folded his arms, and tried to concentrate on what the newscaster was saying, but one long blink turned into another.

## CHAPTER 5

"Where is he?" Dalisay finger combed her hair and draped it over one shoulder. She may have paid extra attention to brushing it. With her work outfit of tight white shirt and short black skirt, she only had so much to work with. She would've added makeup, but that hadn't been in her budget and she felt it too duplicitous if she wore it every time she saw him and then he learned that she usually didn't touch the stuff.

Ina squinted over her shoulder. "It's not going through?"

"I don't know." Dalisay tried the call button again. "Is he even logged on?" *Please answer.* Her nerves had launched an attack all day, she could barely sleep. She was going to "meet" the man from the emails. The man who seemed so sincere, witty, relaxed, and just…fun.

He wrote so descriptively about his family that she'd probably know who they were when—if—she met them. If. The thing between them was just starting.

Or was it just ending?

He didn't answer.

Ina clucked and nudged her out of the seat. Dalisay

37

grudgingly moved, but couldn't say no to Ina. Her mom slid in and punched every button, clicked everything on the screen. She knew less about computers than Dalisay. She'd bought one when she'd moved to Manila, but it'd died a year ago and they'd put the money toward the ever-increasing rent instead of a new one. It was more important they kept their phones.

Ina sat back with a "Huh."

Dalisay checked her phone. Aaron was fifteen minutes late. "Should we just wait?"

"Keep the window up, but you have other Americans to respond to before work."

"I can do that after work."

"Save the money and do it now. Take an Uber home." Ina stuffed a few bills in her apron pocket. Dalisay wanted to argue, but Ina gave her a hard look.

"Yes, Ina."

They switched places, and Dalisay took as much time as she could minimizing the Skype window. *Where are you, Aaron?*

She pulled up her dating account. Three of the men her mom had been fielding had left new messages. One sent oily shivers through Dalisay's body.

She showed Ina the message. "I don't like this one. 'Your skin shines like a million stars lighting up the night sky. I dream of the touch under my fingertips.'"

Ina squinted at the message. "What? It's romantic?"

But with Aaron, it hadn't been about looks. They were getting to know each other. Like how his horse was a gelding named Twitty that was good at something called "cutting" and it meant sorting cattle. He'd played football as a kid, even coached his brothers' middle school teams.

But the older man her mom had bumped did nothing but comment on her looks. She'd rather walk down the street and smile demurely at the catcallers instead of ignoring them than encourage any more messaging with the man.

"What about the other two?" Ina asked.

Good. Ina may not push the creepy American issue.

"One says he retired early and loves to travel." Dalisay wrinkled her nose.

"What's wrong with traveling?" Ina gestured to the computer. "He might not stand you up when you come to work an hour early to talk to him."

"Right." But Dalisay had little interest in traveling. She'd been so excited to move to Manila. Home had equaled prison at times when her dad had been alive, only in the way an impetuous child resents rules of any kind.

Manila had quickly revealed itself to be expensive, crowded, and dangerous. Starbucks, a novelty in her province, had quickly lost its appeal because now there was one on every corner and she couldn't afford it half the time. Ina had gotten mugged within a month of living here, but by then it was too late to turn back. They'd forged ahead. Because while Metro Manila was a force, so was her mother.

The idea of having a home, one where she didn't worry about getting murdered on her way home or being smashed a little too close to the man next to her on the bus, was more appealing than seeing the world. She wasn't in love with Manila like a lot of her old friends from the province.

Dalisay scanned the third American. He was also older than her dad would've been now, with three kids, all in their thirties. He included pictures of his home in the States but didn't mention where he lived.

The house was huge, but that wasn't her concern, either. Some uneasiness sank in at his profile. He was not a healthy-looking man, and while appearances weren't everything, it was hard to adjust to thinking of marrying a man as old as him when she'd been ready to settle with Benjie, a man her age with the agility and virility of someone in their early twenties.

Aaron was twenty-nine, a full thirty years younger than American Three, and he ticked the attractiveness box for her. He was fit, with an active job, and wouldn't leave her a widow after a decade, barring unforeseen accidents.

"Ina, I don't like any of them."

"The one you do like didn't call."

"Something may have come up."

Ina dipped her head in acquiescence. "We don't have time, Dali. Pick another to set up a time to chat with."

No time to wait on Aaron. No time to wonder if he was all right, or if anything she'd written had turned him away. Dalisay chose the traveler, her heart sinking with each word. *Good-bye Aaron W.*

Log this shift as the longest one ever. It was like a dark cloud had followed Dalisay all night. She plastered a fake smile on so her customers wouldn't complain. Finally, she was done. Ina was waiting up.

Dalisay walked to the exit, but then glanced over her shoulder at a row of empty terminals. She had some of her own cash and wouldn't be chewing into Ina's money. Plus, the Uber would be a faster trip than the bus. Maybe.

She trotted to a terminal and logged in.

Aaron W.'s message titled I'M SO SORRY!! jumped out at her.

With a soar of excitement, she pushed her chair back with a grin and pulled it up.

*"I can't believe I missed our call. You have every apology I can make. I got in from working outside all day and watched the news and fell asleep. I'm officially becoming my dad, I guess."*

She giggled. Her dad used to nod off on the rare moments he quit working.

*"I understand if you want to drop me, but just in case, I'm going to wait with my account open. Gimme a call. I'll wait for an hour after you're done with work for good measure."*

She had fifty-five minutes left. Ina would be worried if she took too long.

Was ten minutes too long?

She dialed him.

Her heart careened into her throat when he answered.

"Hi, Daisy."

Oh. Ohhh. Aaron's voice was deep and pleasing, rumbling over her nerves like she'd never experienced. A white wall was behind him and his eyes really were as blue as his picture, his smile hesitant, and his hair…messy. Had he run his hands through it all night worrying about standing her up?

Would that win points with Ina?

"Hello, Aaron." Her smile froze. She hadn't planned on talking to him. What'd she look like? In the little view window, she subtly straightened her long hair over one shoulder. Good thing it was so thick and heavy, or it'd be standing on end like his, only not nearly as adorable.

His expression sobered. "I'm really sorry. Like, really, really sorry. I've been up since two in the morning when I woke up in the recliner."

"The time difference is difficult." Couldn't she come up with anything better? She spoke slower than normal. Knowing English well was one thing, but trying to be coherent when her nerves clambered all over her body was another.

His grin was easy, calming her nerves. "Yes, it is. But look at us, we made it happen. You, actually. How was work?"

Her brows rose at his thoughtfulness. Her ex had never

asked how her day went. In his eyes, she'd dropped out of nursing school and was now a waitress, and that certainly hadn't interested him. "Good. It was a little slower because the students are testing and aren't in using the internet." Her smile wavered. This was nothing like emailing back and forth. This was real. A real man was on the other end. A real man she had to try to marry.

Because American One, Two, and Three couldn't be options. They just couldn't. She felt zero attraction to them, and while her and her mom's situation was dire, they had time. They had to make time. This was Dalisay's life, too.

"Work was good."

He cocked his head. "Good?"

"Yes." She shrunk in on herself. He was just so…so… More. What would he be like in person?

His gaze left the screen. "Let me turn the volume up. I can't hear you."

Probably because she wasn't talking that loud. She never talked loud. Not even when explaining why a mistress was unacceptable.

"I'm sorry. I will speak up. Can you understand me?"

He ducked his head. "Yes. Do you speak, uh, English? Well, I mean obviously you do." He chuckled and tugged a hand through his hair. "I mean all the time."

Was he nervous?

Because she was about to vomit on the floor. Then she'd be really late getting home and wouldn't get paid for cleaning it up.

"Not really. Do you understand me?"

"Oh, you're perfectly clear. I never learned a second language."

She shrugged and smiled because what else did she do? This wasn't quite a date, but it was more intimate than an interview. "I learned it growing up and I watch American television. Many of my university classes were in English."

A knock came from his end. His smile dropped, and he scowled to something beyond the camera. "I'm busy," he called. He glanced back. "Sorry. They're not used to me being late for work, but I had to make sure I was around in case you gave me a second chance."

"It's no problem." Not anymore. But to her mother it was. "Should we talk again another day? I should get home."

She refused to bargain with herself on eking more time out of this conversation. Her mom was probably worrying.

"Of course. Gosh, isn't it late there?"

"Yes." There was no reason to elaborate about how late it was. There were Uber drivers everywhere, so she wouldn't have to wait long once she scheduled one. The indulgence of the car ride could be offset by best utilizing the extra time it gave her.

"I'm sorry. Yes, you'd better get home. Tomorrow? Today? Uh, when we had planned but one day later?" He looked so hopeful. And the warm glow he created when he acted worried about her burned hotter the longer they talked.

"Yes. I'll call you again since I'm at the café."

"Whatever works best for you. Good night, Daisy. And thanks for calling back." His smile was slightly lopsided. Could that have made him any more good-looking?

"Good night, Aaron." She clicked off. Good night? Ugh. It was daytime for him. Good way to end like an idiot.

She checked the time and sprinted out the door. The short conversation had been worth being late over.

AARON SET HIS COMPUTER ASIDE. His grin refused to fade.

Daisy was real. As a person and not a fake profile, and genuine. No one could fake that much nervousness.

She'd been sweet. Timid. But she'd called him, so she didn't let fear stop her. Or was he putting his own hopes into her actions? A good con artist would know how to play him.

Someone rapped on his door again.

"Fucker, open up," Cash yelled from the other side.

Aaron couldn't even be irritated. The tiny beauty on the other end of the computer, on the other end of the world, lit up his entire day.

When he'd woken up last night, he'd panicked when he saw the time. Skype had been as quiet as his house. She'd given up on him and had started her shift.

He managed to keep his apology message short and limited it to one when he wanted to send an apology every five minutes. Staying up the rest of the night, he'd sent a message to his cousins that he had to stick close to home and he'd shut his phone off.

He unlocked the door and pushed out past Cash.

"You look like shit," Cash commented.

He did? He'd been too busy watching Daisy to notice himself in the little box. Ducking into the bathroom didn't help his ego. He looked like shit. Circles from half a night of sleep shone like they were lined with neon lights, and every strand of hair pointed in a different direction.

Daisy must've thought she'd called a madman. And she'd looked so serene. Straightening his hair didn't help now, but it was the only thing he could do even if it was ten minutes too late. She'd gotten a view of the real him, whether that was good or bad.

Cash lingered outside the door, the look on his face like he was evaluating Aaron's sanity. "Did you have girl in your bedroom or what?"

"*No.*" His heart rate kicked up. Had Cash heard Daisy? How would Aaron explain her?

"Who were you talking to, then?"

"No one." He tried to leave the bathroom, but the wall of Cash didn't move.

"Not gonna talk, huh? Why weren't you answering your phone? You leave some cryptic 'I can't be bothered' message and won't return our calls."

"I shut my phone off. I slept like crap last night."

"Because of that girl in your room?"

Aaron scowled. "There is no girl."

Cash pushed off the doorframe and meandered down the hall. "Whatever. You're an adult. I'm just saying that if you did have a girl in that room, you either need to keep her for being brave enough to enter this madhouse, or run because she's just as crazy."

Daisy didn't know about his madhouse so technically, neither option fit. "It's not that bad."

"What'd Trina say when she dumped you?"

Aaron flipped Cash off and went to the fridge to dig out the orange juice. He withdrew the jug. "Nice." It had enough liquid to cover the bottom, maybe a quarter cup. There was no more juice in the fridge, either. Water was the last option.

Cash snorted. "Abbi would kick my ass to Wisconsin and back if I pulled that."

"Yep." Aaron downed the remnants and tossed the jug. "What'd you need?"

"All the cattle are back in the pasture, thanks for asking."

"What?" He'd shut his phone off for a few hours. Why'd Murphy's Law say those few hours were when he'd be needed?

"Eighty head almost made it to the highway. I don't know how those heifers can sniff out the weak points of the fence, but they found it."

Aaron pinched the bridge of his nose. The lack of sleep was bearing down on him like that herd of eighty cows. "Damn. I'm sorry."

"I got ahold of the other guys, after talking Abbi down from saddling her horse. Like I can do any work worrying about my pregnant wife running down pregnant cows. Anyway, one of us decided someone needed to check on you and I drew the short straw."

"Thanks," Aaron said sarcastically.

Cash grinned. "Any time. Seriously, though. Everything okay?"

"Yeah. I'll grab my stuff and head out with you."

"Nope. You stay in bed. I was serious. You look like hell. Take a day and recover from whatever ails you."

Aaron's bed called to him. He hated to miss a day of work, but it was their slow season and if he napped now, he'd be awake for his next chat with Daisy.

# CHAPTER 6

Two weeks of video chatting had gone by. Dalisay twisted her hands nervously and stared at the empty screen.

Ina stood over her shoulder. "You have to ask him today. If he can't fly out to marry you, then we have to move on."

Her mother had been keeping the two non-creepy Americans at bay while Dalisay built a relationship with Aaron. Ina refused to let them go in case Aaron fell through, but one was pressuring Dalisay into agreeing to a visit.

Her anticipation at Aaron's reaction was killing her. It would cost him thousands to travel here and he couldn't stay with them, so housing was an extra expense. Ina leaned over and punched the dial button, then she sidled out of the way.

Aaron's smiling face appeared. His hair was combed, and the yellow lines in his blue plaid collared shirt brought out the color in his eyes. Her stomach flipped like a dancing dolphin. He looked better every time he called.

"How are ya, Daisy?"

Her voice left for a second. That deep rumble of his turned her insides molten.

"Good," she squeaked, too aware of her mom peering at her from a foot away where Aaron couldn't see her. "How are you?"

He chatted about the weather and how they were expanding their herd. His face lit up when he described getting to visit his little nephew. Dalisay would love little nieces and nephews, but she was an only child. Ina said they'd tried, but she hadn't gotten pregnant again.

Ina's stare turned stern. *"Ask him,"* she mouthed.

Dalisay swallowed and directed her gaze back to the screen. "Would you…would you like to come visit?"

His brows lifted. "Oh." She couldn't describe his expression, but now his brows were pinched together. "I suppose we should meet, huh. I mean, not that I don't want to meet you—it just hasn't been that long since we've started talking."

The look of alarm on Ina's face might've matched her own. "No, it hasn't. You're right. I…" She couldn't think of what to say next. "I need to know where this is going," she blurted.

Her mother nodded, but it hadn't felt like the right thing to say. She should've said something complimentary, something other than the truth. But in the end, it was the truth. She couldn't string herself along on Aaron W. if they weren't heading to the altar.

And as much as she'd gotten on board with the plan to marry and move overseas, she wasn't going to sacrifice her entire life to do it. Otherwise, why not move home and hit up Michael? Then she'd still be around her family, like her mom, who could coast through life with her.

The more she thought about America and researched its schools and opportunities, the more she envisioned herself there. She could get her own car, live in a city that wasn't as populated as Metro Manila, and apply for scholarships to university. Each time she talked to Aaron, she crushed on him harder. She was definitely in like with him. That made it all the more critical that they meet. Because if he wasn't in it for the long haul, or their chemistry was off, she'd have to scramble to find another suitable bachelor. Or move back to the province and forget her dreams forever.

Aaron hadn't said much about the town he lived in, just that Moore was a small town but within driving distance to a couple of bigger cities. How perfect was that?

"This would be the best time of year for me to travel." His expression was unsure, but he watched her like he gauged her reaction.

"I could send you a list of decent hotels in my area." It wouldn't matter with Manila traffic. It'd still take a couple of hours to commute to get there. She lifted a shoulder, afraid anything she'd say would push him into deciding not to come.

"I don't know how long I could stay, but I'd like to see you."

"However long will be fine." As long as they married while he was here.

Her hands trembled. She clutched them in her lap. During her engagement, she hadn't been as nervous as this.

They talked more with her mother watching. It brought her back to the days of dating when Ina would accompany her on dates for the first few weeks until she vetted him. With few good friends, there had been no one else to go along.

Dalisay was about to say goodbye when he gave a firm nod. "All right. I'll send you the flight information when I have it." His smile was hesitant. "I look forward to seeing you, Daisy."

~

AARON PUT ALL his tools away by tossing them on the workbench. Good enough. He'd finished putting a new belt in his favorite combine. They had three, but he babied this one. It was one of the first major pieces of equipment he and his cousins bought after they'd taken over. It was a luxury liner compared to the older combines he'd grown up using. Since then, they'd upgraded the other two with newer used models and he did some of the easier tasks Brock didn't have time for.

The sound of an engine reached the large shop where he kept two of the combines and one of the semis. The guys were showing up. Another pickup droned with the first. Aaron stepped out of the shop. Travis had already parked, and Brock had ridden with Cash and Dillon.

Now was the time. Mom and Dad were waiting inside with his brothers. Aaron had asked them over to discuss his plans.

A trip to Manila would be a considerable expense. The plane tickets cost as much as he'd feared, along with the hotel Daisy recommended. The money wasn't what worried him. Neither was the time away.

No, he absolutely stressed about the time away.

Would Nicolas get in trouble with Emily's parents while he was gone? Which cousin was going to be away from his budding family and hauling grain while Aaron kicked it in paradise? And his parents? Would they have the fight that ended it all since he wouldn't be around to set up distractions for them? All it'd take was Dad turning the channel before the *Wheel of Fortune* puzzle was solved.

Yeah, he'd have to leave a chore schedule for his brothers and maybe his parents while he was at it.

Telling his family why he was going to be gone ate a hole right through his stomach lining. He was almost thirty and Daisy was twenty-three. They were both adults; it shouldn't be a problem. But how did one break the news that he was flying overseas to meet the woman he might marry, only he hadn't met her in person yet?

No matter what they thought, he was flying out next week. He'd haul a load of soybeans to the elevator on Monday and he'd fly out Tuesday. Over twenty-four hours of travel time. When was the last time he'd sat still for that long?

Dragging in an icy breath, he tucked his face into his coat collar and crunched through the snow-crusted gravel toward his house. He couldn't even take his time walking across the yard. The wind cut through his skin and down to the bone until the bridge of his nose stung like he had brain freeze without the fun of a bowl of ice cream.

The guys had been curious when Aaron had asked them to come solo. He loved their spouses, but this topic was too personal. In a way, he wanted to meet with just the ladies and listen to their thoughts on the subject and how they thought the others would handle the news. He hadn't because what if it hadn't been positive? Elle was practical to a fault. Abbi might fist-bump him and say "go for it." Josie would stay out of it because she wouldn't want to ruffle the waters after how she and Brock had gotten their start. And then there was Kami. The wild card to Travis's efficient speculation of all the reasons why this wouldn't work.

He hadn't considered telling the rest of his cousins, the ones he didn't work with. The information was going to spread like an autumn grass fire and he'd have enough opinions lobbed at him.

Voices drifted out from the house. Loud guffaws as his family combined into the moderately sized living room. They used to get together more often, but after his dad and uncles sold and all of them moved, the frequency had dwindled. Aaron and the rest didn't hang out as often as they had in the past because they weren't five bachelors looking for a good time. Aside from a few holiday get-togethers every year, they just kept an open-door policy and visited when the occasion arose.

He entered into the familiar warmth and mess of his mudroom. Savory scents surrounded him, and his stomach ditched its mess of nerves long enough to rumble, reminding him he hadn't eaten much for breakfast. It was only noon, but a pot roast simmered in the crockpot, Jackson's favorite kitchen gadget. Set it and forget it. Aaron had no food or appetizers to serve his visitors; he hadn't been sure anyone would be staying.

"We're all here, Aaron," Mom called from where they were all crowded. "Time to break the bad news."

Aaron paused taking his boots off. *Thanks for the foreboding, Mom.* Hopefully, she wouldn't think his news was bad. He slung his jacket on top of the pile, but kept his Walker Five cap on.

"Yeah, we're dying to know," Cash said. "And by we, I mean Abbi."

Aaron grinned in spite of the inferno raging within. He entered the room. No seats were available. His brothers sat together on the short couch and thumbed through their phones. Aaron wouldn't be surprised if they were messaging each other. Dillon was in the corner, murmuring with Dad. Poor Dillon always got grilled about all the work planned and where Dad could lend a hand. If Dillon minded, he never let on. Travis would be targeted next. Dad was as interested as the rest of them in upcoming trends and what the Walker Five planned to incorporate. When Travis had brought a drone home to check crops and fence line, Dad had been the closest to giddy as Aaron had ever seen.

Cash and Brock were pinned by Mom as she extracted all the latest happenings in their homes. Cash gladly discussed

Abbi and how she was feeling as she neared her due date. Brock's answers were short, but Mom knew to keep asking questions until she was satisfied.

"Thanks for coming." The room quieted down. They all looked at him, except for Jackson and Nicolas, who barely glanced up from their phones.

"I'm going to leave on Tuesday. I'll be gone for almost three weeks."

That did the trick. He had all of their attention. Him leaving town was an oddity. Three weeks was unheard of.

"Whatever you need, man," Dillon replied, as if he sensed the gravity in Aaron's voice.

Aaron nodded his thanks. If only Dillon kept that attitude for the next few minutes. "I met a woman online and we're going to meet in person."

That little tidbit dropped like a Fourth of July smoke bomb. A spark to ignite and then a steady infusion of shock.

"Where's she from?" Travis asked. Leave it to him to suss out the gap in information.

"The Philippines," Aaron answered. He rushed to get the real shocker out so it didn't keep spinning like a cyclone in his brain. "She lives in Manila. If it goes well, we'll probably get married."

Someone snorted. Probably Nicolas. Or Cash.

"Married?" The blue in Mom's hazel eyes sparkled with incredulity. "To a girl you haven't met yet?"

"Like a mail-order bride?" Nicolas asked. Everyone swung their head toward his brother, then back at him.

"No. We've been talking and stuff." Aaron shoved his hands in his pockets.

"That's all you can do with an ocean between you," Cash drawled.

Aaron scowled at him. "Her name is Daisy." She wasn't both nameless and faceless to them now.

"Daisy what?" Mom asked.

"Dalisay Calamba Cortez."

"And she goes by Daisy?"

Aaron grounded his teeth together. "She said she likes when I call her Daisy. It was her profile name."

Jackson coughed a laugh. "And what was yours? Lonely Farmer with Money?"

Aaron scowled at his brother. The tension in the room thickened. Jackson only said what others were thinking. "I'm not rushing headlong into this. I've done some research and got a passport. We're meeting first and if there's something between us, then I can come back and apply for a visa for her."

"How…" Mom blinked and looked away, her mouth working. "How did you meet her?"

Brock spoke. "He said online."

Irritation flashed through Mom's features, but softened when she glanced at Brock. "I mean, what site? Did you really go looking for a mail-order bride?"

"She's not a mail-order bride. I went looking for someone to start a relationship with. Someone who'd be willing to get to know the real me." He gave Jackson a pointed look. "Unlike the women in town who *do* know how well off our family is. Look at you all. Married. Having kids." While he was raising the family that'd raised him. "If I haven't found anyone in Moore, then it's not happening."

"Why the Philippines?" Dad asked.

"Why not?" Aaron tried not to be defensive but the conversation thus far had done nothing to ease his mind that he'd worried about nothing.

"Well, why international, for one," Travis said. "Why not Tinder around Fargo and meet a girl who's familiar with forty below zero weather?"

"Because that girl still might not want to share her life

with a guy whose job is his life." He glanced at Cash. "What'd Abbi think of your first calving season?"

Cash rubbed the back of his neck. "I'll admit, she had her first 'What did I get myself into?' moment, but it's not like she was going to leave me over it. And the first googly eyed calf she had to bottle feed sealed the deal in case I hadn't."

But Cash's parents didn't live with him.

"Why the Philippines?" Travis asked again. "And not Russia, or... Where else do they do mail—international dating?"

"I looked around." It still seemed seedy to say that. Too close to *shopped around*. "I read a lot of success stories and a ton of failure stories. I mean, it can be bad—for either party, but mostly for the women. I found a dating site that seemed more likely to have couples looking for long-lasting love."

Mom started to say something, then huffed out a breath. She ran a hand through her wavy hair that was getting grayer with each year that went by. "I don't understand her perspective. Is life so bad that she has to marry a stranger?"

He shook his head. "Not at all." Daisy hadn't said so. "Her dad passed away and it's just her and her mom. She said she'd been in school for nursing when her dad died, and she'd had to drop out."

"So it's a money thing?" Mom asked.

"No." He took his hat off and ran a hand through his hair. This wasn't going well. "I mean, why do we go to the bar? We go to meet people because love might happen there when it hasn't happened at church, or at work, or wherever. Think of this dating site as a bar. We met, we started talking, we liked each other."

"You said you were going to marry her," Brock pointed out.

"That's what I'm flying to the Philippines for. To meet her

before we make the leap. How long did you know Josie before you wanted to marry her?"

"We met a week before the Fourth of July parade, then—"

"My point is that you didn't know her long. I've already been chatting with Daisy for over a month. We haven't even kissed, and I know her better than any other person I've dated."

The room went quiet. Had that finally gotten through to them? He didn't want to leave with everyone intent on changing his mind.

His dad spoke first. "It still seems a bit extreme. And like her only goal is to get her green card."

"She could do that quicker than waiting on me. I just want to meet her. Who knows, we might not be compatible and you'll all be right."

"We don't want to be right about this not working out," Travis said. "We don't want to see you get hurt."

The others nodded. Except Mom. She gave him a steady stare with the slight crease between her brows that meant she hadn't given her approval about anything.

"You're sure you're not planning to marry her over there?" Mom asked in a stern tone.

"No. I'd want all of you at the wedding. And I don't want to marry and then fly home while she sits and waits for a visa." He wanted a real wedding, with all his family and the town to celebrate, to prove to everyone that the relationship was serious and not bought and paid for. "And you all know I can't be away for months."

Her mouth flattened. "There's that then. I don't like it, but I'll reserve judgment until you meet her in person."

Dad cleared his throat. "So you two decide to… You get home, and then what?"

"We apply for the visa and she'll fly over when it goes

through. We'd have ninety days to get married or she'd have to go back."

The information didn't soften the lines in Dad's forehead. "And during that window is when you'd get married?"

Aaron nodded.

Cash folded his arms, his expression serious. "The time between you flying home and her coming here? What would she be doing?"

They obviously didn't trust her. Aaron sighed and pinched the bridge of his nose. The line of tension radiating through the room had broken. He didn't want to snap it back in place, but he had to draw a line. "I guess that's between her and I."

His cousins gave him assessing looks, like they were deciding if they should respect his limits.

It didn't matter. If he and Daisy were going to get over the hurdle of how they met, it would be together, not him making excuses to everyone.

"I want you to call when you get there," Mom demanded. "And check in every day."

Aaron suppressed a sigh. "I'll call when I land and as often as I can. I'll be all right."

"I'll take over for you while you're gone. Just go over what you need done." Dad sounded slightly less disturbed about the situation than Mom.

Aaron nodded. He had it all mapped out and ready; he just had to find the scrap of paper he'd scribbled it all on. Was it in the shop or his office?

He tapped the front pocket of his flannel button-up. The fabric crinkled. Good thing he hadn't tossed his shirt in the wash yet. He dug it out and handed it to Dad. He hated bogging the guy down in retirement. Dad needed a hobby other than watching cable shows he'd missed all the years he'd been in the field.

"I'd appreciate it if you guys keep this to yourselves as much as possible. I don't want her showing up and everyone thinking she's a mail-order bride. I'd rather she got to town and then we told everyone that she and I met online." Then it'd look like they'd been dating a while before the wedding. If the town caught wind of the juicy gossip first, he feared Daisy would be labeled and feel more like a fish out of water than she might otherwise.

"If it works out," his mom added.

Yeah. If it worked out.

# CHAPTER 7

$\mathcal{A}$aron shot a text off as soon as he got the all clear to turn on cellular service after landing. He'd upgraded phone plans but informed his family he was sticking to texts. It didn't stop him from compiling and elaborating on his to-do list for his dad. Aaron reiterated the times and contacts for the grain hauls. Little had changed since the day Dad had ran his share of the farm, but he didn't do it every day anymore.

Another text was sent to each brother. Meal nights, reminders to behave, and as many extra chores that Aaron could think of to keep them out of trouble and out of their parents' hair. To Mom, he sent the dates and times of the boys' conferences and vacation days. All he'd need was for one or both of his brothers to sleep in and miss school right before Thanksgiving vacation was to start.

He strode off the plane, grateful to stretch his legs and back. It was…what day now? He'd left on Tuesday and traveled for an entire day. It was now Wednesday evening in Manila. To his internal clock, it was Wednesday morning and the shoddy sleep he'd gotten on the plane didn't equate a full night of rest. Daisy had offered to meet him, but if his flight was delayed, he didn't want her to hang around the airport. And he'd be more rumpled than usual after the flight. She'd assured him that he could get an Uber and language wouldn't be a problem.

He checked his watch. She'd be starting her shift soon. They were meeting for lunch the next day, giving him some time to sleep off the jet lag. Her mom would accompany her to have lunch at the hotel. According to the stories he'd read, it would be typical for Daisy to bring a friend or relative to their first few meetings. It was smart, too.

The Manila airport had wide corridors and a sleek, modern look. He'd only flown a few times before, but this was his first international trip. Did he look as out of place as he felt?

He glanced down at his wrinkled white T-shirt and unbuttoned plaid flannel that hung over faded blue jeans. The hard soles of his work boots didn't make much noise. Had he even packed a pair of athletic shoes?

The travel fog in his mind blocked any memory of what he'd packed. He wound his way to baggage claim, thankful that the main points of the airport process were similar in different countries.

Suitcase in hand, he rolled it behind him to track down a ride to his hotel. Warm, muggy air swamped him as soon as he cleared the door. It wasn't as bad as he expected, but this wasn't the worst time of year.

He looked around. Definitely not Minnesota. The other day he was in a grain truck, cruising along the wide-open expanse of the highway. No snow had stuck around back home, but the fields were all harvested and brown. Tonight, he was surrounded by concrete, people, and buildings taller than any that could be found in Moore.

Since he was a beacon for "I need a ride," he was invited

right into a taxi. The driver sped off and Aaron clutched the edge of the seat. Fast-paced music filled the cab, and Aaron hunkered down to watch the scenery fly by. Traffic plugged the roads. The surreal experience could just as well have happened to another person. They passed other taxis, other taxis passed them, and a thrill coursed through him whenever he passed a real Jeepney. He was pushed back into his seat when the taxi's speed picked up in four lanes, then bumped back and forth when they hit stop and go traffic.

All his internet research was alive and more real than he imagined it could be—and faster paced. He didn't care if he was the definition of touristy, he gawked out the window. Brightly colored signs were a blur through the window and the honking was constant. Some high-rises were obviously residential, with small patios lining the sides from top to bottom. He hoped they would be arriving at his hotel soon, as the buildings grew even taller and were covered in glass, but it still took several minutes to reach his destination. His eyelids were getting hard to keep open, but the scenery was too fascinating to miss. Finally, the driver pulled into an arched entryway.

Aaron fumbled through paying the driver, and by the time he was done, both he and his luggage stood in front of a set of glass doors.

Hell, this was the fanciest place he'd ever stayed. Check-in went smoothly, and he found his room. Dropping his bag inside the door, he flipped the lock and sauntered to the window.

Aside from vacations as a kid to Disney World and his few trips to Minneapolis, this was by far the biggest metropolis he'd ever been to. Talk about feeling like a hick.

Which wasn't a bad thing. Unless Daisy thought so.

This was her home? Bright lights, chaotic streets, and neon signs as far as he could see.

Where'd she live compared to here? She'd said this was the closest quality hotel she could find.

He turned away from the window. From the walnut wood accents to the flat screen TV and the fluffy white comforter on the king-sized bed, he couldn't tell he was in a different country.

A wave of weariness propelled his feet toward the bed. He collapsed facedown on it and let his eyes drift shut.

A CACOPHONOUS RINGING ROUSED AARON. He popped his head up and winced. A kink had formed in his neck while he slept. Blinking against the wall of light shining through the wall-to-wall windows, he struggled to recall where he was.

The ringing stopped. His eyes shot wide.

Daisy! What time was it? He scrambled to look around for the phone. The cordless sat on the small table by the TV cabinet. He willed it ring again. No luck.

Dammit. He twisted onto his back and winced as his tight muscles protested.

"Fuck." According to his phone in Manila time, it was ten minutes after he was supposed to meet Daisy.

Popping off the bed, he strode toward the door. They were supposed to meet in the lobby. Daisy would take him around the corner to a cheaper place to eat, one she claimed wouldn't price gouge the traveler as badly.

The phone's ring stopped him in a heartbeat. He spun on his heel and raced for the room phone.

"Hey," he answered, breathless, but fully alert thanks to the adrenaline racing through his veins.

"Aaron. Hi. I…was afraid you didn't make it." The upbeat tone of her voice didn't mask the concern underlying it. Had she worried he'd stood her up?

"I fell asleep in my room less than five minutes after being here. I didn't think I'd conk out so hard, otherwise I would've set an alarm. Are you in the lobby?"

"Yes. Ina and I are here."

"Be down in five." He clicked off at her "Bye" and dove for his suitcase. After tossing it on the bed, he whipped out a fresh set of clothes. Wrinkled, but better than what he had on. Daisy might as well see it now before he was accused of false advertising.

He frowned as he ripped out of his current clothing and tugged on the fresh set. This wasn't how he wanted to meet her in person. The blue pinstriped button-up wasn't the outfit he'd chosen for lunch. He'd picked his church clothes for that: crisp white shirt and black jeans. He wouldn't even wear his hat.

His hat.

Running a hand through his hair, he searched for a mirror.

Hell. A cap was needed more than a pair of pants. With one, he'd have a hailstorm's chance in hell of hiding the dark circles under his eyes and the unruly nest perched on top of his head.

Hadn't he made an appointment to get a haircut?

His stomach plummeted. Yes. He'd made it for last weekend and forgot about the damn thing as soon as he'd hung up the phone. Now he was shaggy, and he'd stiffed some poor girl out of twenty bucks plus tip.

There wasn't time to dwell on it. He had two more minutes to speed to the lobby but he barely remembered what floor he was on and where the elevators were. Snagging the key card off the bathroom counter, he breezed out his door. The elevator was easy enough to find.

It was empty when the doors opened. He shuffled inside and pushed the button for the main floor.

His heart thrummed, slowing down now that he was on his way to Daisy as fresh as he could be. Leaning his head back, he let his eyelids drift closed. As the elevator pinged for the lobby, he popped his eyes open.

Oh. Shit. The ceiling of the elevator car was mirrored and he'd forgotten his cap. He never forgot his cap. Because he had an extra in his truck, his shop, and five hanging by the front door.

His only cap in the Philippines was the one he wore on the flight and it was lying on the bed where he'd chucked it. Perfect.

Frantically finger combing his hair as he exited the elevator, he wished he could pull off the disheveled look like his brothers, but they spent too long in the bathroom trying to achieve that appearance. His gaze swept the bustling, open layout.

White marble and gold accents made the lobby seem larger than it was. Couples in power suits and heels marched back and forth. Hotel clerks checked guests in at the desk, a congenial smile on each of their faces. He recalled the friendly atmosphere from yesterday. It'd put him at ease after the road trip that was unlike any he'd ever taken. Once the fifth motorcyclist had zipped between his cab and the car next to him, he'd quit flinching.

Movement in the lounge area of the lobby caught his eye. A woman with long, jet-black hair draped over one shoulder stood up.

His breath froze. Daisy.

Her skin glowed under the lighting of the lounge chandelier, and she tipped her head to the side as she considered him. Dark eyes that he knew to be the softest brown evaluated him. Her gaze drifted over his hair, and he swallowed hard. He should've taken another few minutes and gone back for his cap. No, he was late enough. She didn't deserve to wait. Her smile was slow and hesitant as she met his gaze.

His world stopped, but somehow his feet kept moving. The grown man in him acknowledged that he wanted to run. He'd never been on a date that tied him in knots like this. For senior high prom, he'd gone with a good friend. The rest of his dates he'd met at the bar, or through his friends and cousins.

He hadn't "met" Daisy yet. While they'd chatted through the computer, she'd still been unreal. But now they were in the same room, and she was *very* real. From her thick glossy hair, to her plain purple top tucked into a pair of white pants she wore like a second skin and shoes that Nicolas's girlfriend called Converses. She was the girl next door that grew up an ocean away. And that he might marry.

He was almost to her. If he didn't change course, he'd run into the back of one of the couches. Another lady rose next to Daisy, and for all that Daisy was short, this woman was even more petite, and her look much shrewder.

That must be Ina. He sifted through his brain for her name—Mari. That was it! Daisy had only told him once. She always called her mom Ina.

Mari narrowed her gaze on him. She scrutinized him from his hair down to his scuffed boots. His nicer pair was packed away or scattered on the bed with everything else; he couldn't recall.

"Finally, we meet." He grinned. Couldn't help it. Because he had no idea how to act, he shoved his hands into his pockets and threaded through the furniture until he stood in front of Daisy and her mother.

Hugging would be too forward, but he wanted to. His curiosity was insatiable about how her slender build would tuck into him. The top of her head hit below his shoulders, the perfect height to nuzzle into her hair. Did she use a fruity shampoo, or one with a floral scent? Would her hair be as soft as it looked?

He took his hands out of his pockets, almost reached for her, but kept them at his side.

"Daisy." He nodded at her, then her mom. "May I call you Mari?"

"Yes." Mari's expression hadn't wavered since she'd first set eyes on him. Her hair was pulled back, her eyes a slightly lighter shade of brown than Daisy's warm hickory tones.

Daisy said her mom learned English as a kid but didn't speak it often. He'd do his best to learn their language, but he'd taken two years of Spanish in high school and probably couldn't order a cup of coffee without needing someone to translate for him. He wasn't likely to do well learning her language.

"Hello, Aaron." Daisy's shy smile made him smile again and there they stood, grinning at each other while Mari checked the time.

Mari spoke to Daisy, her tone stern. Daisy nodded and looked at him, a shadow of guilt crossing her face. "I'm sorry, but I have to work in a few hours. Do you mind if we go to lunch right away?"

Her voice was like satin. In their chats, she'd been soft spoken. She still was, but in person, she was...better. In every way.

"Come," she said to him, but grasped her mom's elbow. "What kind of food do you like?"

"The usual. A burger and fries is fine. I like steak and mashed potatoes. My brother makes a killer beef stroganoff. I don't mind pasta as long as there's meatballs." He chuckled, suddenly nervous at the perplexed look on her face. "Rancher food, I guess."

"Um...perhaps we try..."

Mari spoke to Daisy again and her tone said it all. They weren't going to a place that had rancher food.

"The hotel would have food that you like," Daisy said. "But it's really expensive."

He'd be paying for everything. It was the norm for would-be grooms when they traveled to see their future brides. And God, that's what he was. A would-be groom.

"You know what? When in Rome. Show me what I've been missing out on in Moore, Minnesota."

A smile of relief lit up Daisy's eyes as they walked next to each other. Mari looked between them both, as if rating their sincerity.

Stepping out into the air shocked his system. Yesterday, he had to wear his winter coat and gloves, and it wasn't even the coldest months of the year. Here it was summer again. Only stickier and, his gaze swept the sidewalks, much more crowded.

The sidewalks by the hotel were wide enough for them to walk side by side. As he'd been driven up last night, he'd noticed that traversing around Metro Manila could be a harrowing endeavor if he found himself in an unfamiliar place. Speeding traffic, dubious walkways, and congestion were a recipe for disaster for the ignorant.

"How was your flight?" Daisy asked.

"Long. But no delays. I must've run myself too hard in the days before the trip, getting ready to be gone for so long. I slept over thirteen hours in the same position." But all his aches and pains had vanished. Daisy's presence next to him left him wired.

For being so tiny, they walked at a brisk pace that kept him rushing to keep up.

Mari motioned to a place on their right. Daisy shook her head, but Mari gave her the look, the one he used to get from his mother before she'd quit caring about everything.

Daisy scanned around them and gestured to a place across the street with a green sign. The area outside had a reserved spot for tables and chairs, but they were all packed.

Mari said, "Too busy," and spun toward the door of the first option.

"I'm game for anything," he told Daisy. "Really. It's fine."

Daisy's brows were creased as she glared at her mom's back. She lifted her gaze to him and gave him an apologetic look.

What was that about?

What was Ina up to? This place served nothing but seafood and little of what Aaron would find in his hometown. She'd hoped to coax her mother to the place that imitated an American sports bar, but under the guise of a time limit, Ina chose here.

She led Aaron inside.

He was a big man. His broad shoulders had blocked out the sun for her, but he wasn't intimidating. He couldn't be with that smile of his. The hue of his eyes had startled her in the hotel, but out in the sun, they glowed. As they'd walked, he'd turned the heads of everyone passing.

Was his russet hair purposefully styled in a messy manner, or had he just woken up when she called? The ten-minute wait before she'd decided to call had killed her. Truthfully, she and Ina had been there for over a half hour before. Traffic wasn't going to ruin the big meet.

For a moment, when he'd walked off the elevator, she'd regretted calling him. He towered over her, and he hadn't been standing anywhere close to her. He was so much better looking in real life. His lanky frame helped settle the chaotic swirl of emotions in her belly. He was a wall of muscle, but not cosmetic muscle. He was a man who moved easily, like a dance around everyone and everything, confident in his body. She hadn't expected that from someone well over six feet tall and wearing thick boots.

His feet were going to burn up if he did any walking around Manila.

They were seated at a little table by the window; she and Ina on one side, Aaron on the other. The waitress was about her age and she eyed Aaron like a meat stick she wanted to gnaw apart.

Aaron seemed clueless as he nodded his thanks and crinkled his brow at the menu. So, points in his favor. If there was a discreet way to show her mom that, she'd kick her under the table and point it out.

Ina had kept the contact going with American Two. "He's from Malibu!" she'd said only this morning. Ina was most excited about his mention of a vacation home in the Philippines. American Two now had several points in his favor. Well off, nice house—mansion, and if Daisy went with him, she wouldn't be away for long periods of time.

"I really like Aaron," Daisy had said.

"We hardly know him," she'd replied.

*You don't, but I do.* She'd have to prove it and intervene when Ina tried to get him out of his comfort zone.

What was Ina expecting? That he'd stomp out like a diva once he had to eat the same food she'd grown up on?

"What are you having, Ina?" Daisy asked in English. The crease hadn't left Aaron's forehead.

"Shrimp with oyster sauce." Ina set her menu aside and took a sip of her water. She appeared to be looking outside, but was studying Aaron.

"Ah…" Aaron gave the menu one last scowl. "I'm afraid I need some help with this."

His sheepish smile uncoiled a place inside she'd forgotten existed. The search for a husband had been clinical until she'd bumped Aaron, then it'd been full of uncertainty and urgency but with a healthy dose of excitement. Yet that crush feeling now was like comparing the power of a motorbike to a Jeepney.

She leaned over the table and straightened his menu so she could read it to him. Her fingers brushed his and a zing of electricity traveled up her arm and straight to her belly. He was warm. And real. And here with her.

He glanced up. She caught a quickly concealed flash of heat.

Her mouth went dry, but she forced herself to speak. She started by reading the name of the dish and the description, but as his eyes gradually widened she switched tactics. "Why don't we narrow it down. Do you like fish, shrimp, shellfish, or squid?"

"Squid? For real?"

The sigh from Ina was barely audible.

"Yes, it's real," Dalisay said. "Ina and I love shrimp and shellfish. Yellow tuna is good, too. Do you like spicy food?"

"I don't know that I've had the chance to get to like it. Did you say one of these was tilapia? We have that at home. Why don't I play it safe today, but I gotta try squid before I leave."

"The tilapia shouldn't be too spicy for you, and I can recommend a good squid dish." She met his gaze and the corner of his mouth lifted.

She couldn't help her smile. Neither could she move away. Her arms stayed stretched across the table, her hands spread across his menu while his hands rested next to hers. They weren't even touching, but the intimacy of the moment wasn't lost on her.

Their server appeared, standing closer to Aaron, and she spoke in English. To him only. "What can I get you?"

Aaron didn't break his gaze away. "Can you help me out again?"

Dalisay sat back and ordered for him and Ina. What was she going to eat? She named a dish from when she'd read them off to Aaron.

When the server left after one last sultry glance tossed toward Aaron, which he didn't seem to notice, he asked what she'd ordered.

"Bangsilog. It's milk fish with fried rice and fried egg. It's a breakfast dish, but this is my first meal so it works." Other than the small heart attack he'd given her earlier when he didn't answer her call, his first impression eased her anxiety that he wouldn't be another Benjie.

"Now I feel really bad that I slept in and made you wait."

"No. Don't." It was worth it.

Ina cut in. "Tell us about your work."

Dalisay bristled at Ina's demand, but it didn't faze him. "I farm with four of my cousins. Technically, we own the Walker Five, but more and more of our family is getting involved." His grin was lopsided and his blue eyes twinkled. "We have them as employees now, for better or for worse."

He rattled off information Dalisay already knew. Ina already knew, too, but Dalisay expected the interrogation. Since Richard was Ina's top pick, Aaron wasn't going to get off easy during the times they were together.

When he drifted off, Ina lobbed another question at him. "Are you close to your family?"

His smile faded, and he nodded. "Yes. We're close. Too close sometimes." His chuckle didn't sound as relaxed as it had before.

Ina peppered him with questions she knew the answers to. Aaron responded patiently and didn't comment when Ina misspoke or fumbled over an English phrase. Ina could probably start the process again and Aaron wouldn't flinch.

Their meals were delivered. Aaron's plate was slid in front of him. He pressed back into his chair and stared at the fish on his plate.

After a moment he leaned forward, his blue eyes twinkled as he studied the dish from eyeballs to tail. The outside was blackened from roasting with seasoning sprinkled over the exterior. A cut had been made along the side after cooking to insert lemon slices and springs of rosemary. "I wasn't expecting the entire fish."

"How else would you eat fish?" Ina asked, her tone borderline snide.

Dalisay wanted to sigh. Ina hadn't stumbled over any of those words.

"Filets." Another good-natured laugh. "Go to any café in town and I doubt you'll find fish that hasn't been battered and deep fried. But when the guys and I go fishing, we filet the meat and dump the rest."

Ina scoffed and Dalisay froze. Aaron's gaze lifted to her mother, his eyes full of question.

"Do you ever make fish head soup?" Dalisay asked to cover the awkwardness. As if American Two—Richard—ever saw a fish outside of a grocery store. He didn't seem the type to traipse through the outdoors in the polo shirt and visor he wore in his profile.

Aaron, on the other hand, she could see fishing in the crystal-blue lakes of Minnesota that had popped up in her research.

"No. Is that a thing? It sounds…uh, different." He picked up his fork and pulled back the skin to dig out the meat inside.

Dalisay shot a glance at Ina. What had Aaron been about to say? Disgusting? Delicious? Probably not. Had Ina caught his sudden change?

The not-so-subtle lift of Ina's brow said yes, she'd caught it.

Dalisay's stomach demanded food though her appetite had nose-dived when Aaron's dish had appeared. She gathered some rice on her spoon and snuck a glance at Aaron. He chewed his fish, but his attention was on her mother's plate.

Ina cracked shrimp and peeled the shell off. She popped the meat in her mouth and attacked another. Aaron's gaze stayed on the discarded shell, with tiny black eyeballs still intact.

He seemed enamored over the fish with scales and shrimp with shells. Was his food always stripped bare before it reached his plate? Well, Minnesota was touted for fishing, but they lacked shrimp.

"Want to try one?" Ina asked, holding a shrimp out to him. Damn, she'd caught him staring.

He set his fork down. Dalisay steeled herself for a disgusted look that didn't come. "Do you mind? I don't often eat shrimp, and I've never seen them…like that."

He peeled the shrimp and took a bite. Dalisay and Ina were riveted to his reaction until he swallowed.

"Not bad." He blinked. "Wow. The flavor is so not what I expected. I guess that's the difference between having the ocean right here versus half a country away."

Ina switched to Filipino. "Hear that? You can say goodbye to quality seafood if you stay with him. Malibu is on the ocean."

Aaron looked between them. Dalisay didn't elaborate on what her mother had said, and he went back to his own food. He was more tactful than her mother.

They finished their food in silence. Aaron was done first and studied his surroundings. She tried to put herself in his place. Everything was different, from the language, to the people, to the storefronts, and the cars on the street. Sure, there were similarities. People were still people no matter how they dressed. An engine was an engine no matter what body was built around it, and a store sold goods. But like the fish head soup, it was different. Soon enough, she would be in considerably larger shoes. New culture. New land. New husband.

At that thought, she set her spoon and fork down. She'd been intent to marry before. But she'd known Benjie, or she thought she had. The idea of marriage now was more startling than before. Where she'd known Benjie for months, she'd just spent an hour and a half with Aaron.

The time. She peeked at her phone. "I am sorry. I have to start the commute to work."

Aaron nodded. "Absolutely. Just tell me when and where we meet next."

"I work through the weekend, but we can keep meeting for lunch. On my days off before you leave"—she dragged in a deep breath—"we can go to the province where I'm from and meet my family."

The corner of his mouth lifted in a grin. "Should I be scared?"

She giggled and ignored the sharp look her mother gave her. "No. Ina and I will protect you."

He developed a full grin and pulled out his wallet. "I'm gonna need a little help again."

Dalisay walked him through paying and gave him pointers on tipping and what he should expect to pay for when and if he ventured into Manila on his own. He listened intently, but his gaze would touch on her hair, then drift to a shoulder before jerking back to her eyes. Was he trying not to check her out?

They walked outside into the bustle of sidewalk traffic. Ina murmured that they should take off from there, but Dalisay refused to abandon Aaron in the city by himself on his first outing. He might look like he could take care of himself, but he'd come here for her. They hadn't directly said the word "marriage" to each other, but it was assumed on the dating site they had used. They'd alluded to it with his trip here. She was growing protective of him without an official engagement.

The hotel loomed in front of them, a wall of reflective glass. The location was farther away from her apartment than was convenient, but he'd get a quality room and service for the price. He was close enough to the heart of Metro Manila to play tourist, but not too far that she couldn't catch the bus to meet with him.

"This place is really nice," he said as if reading her mind. "And the weather definitely isn't this pleasant at home. The wind is probably over fifteen miles an hour and will nip a layer of skin off." He stopped, a beat of alarm gleaming through his eyes. "I don't want to scare you off. You get used to it."

So marriage was on his mind, too. "I'm sure it'll be a trade. Typhoons for blizzards. Are they really that bad?" Her heart had pounded when she'd cruised through images of snow-obscured trees, drifts taller than some vehicles, and gigantic trucks tipped into snow-packed ditches.

"Yes and no. Modern amenities decrease the deadliness, but we all strive not to get stuck in one and to be prepared when one hits."

She was about to ask more questions when Ina nudged her. Right. Work. "Well, enjoy the rest of your day."

He smiled, and the corners of his eyes crinkled. "I'll probably check in on my brothers and poke around the hotel. When can I see you next?"

"Ina and I can come for lunch again."

Ina crossed her arms and shook her head. She didn't use English. "We can't afford this bus trip every day."

Dalisay didn't speak in English, either. She didn't want Aaron dragged into the middle. "I can use my tips."

"For groceries. For the power bill. Bus fare for both of us for every day he's here is going to add up."

It wouldn't be both of them for long. Was Ina going to be obstinate about Richard and make sure she stayed between her and Aaron long after he'd proven he was no predator?

Probably.

"Is something wrong?" Aaron asked. The smile had faded, and his concern was directed at her.

"Ina worries the bus fare will be too much."

"Oh, that's my fault. Here." He dug out his wallet and dipped inside. "How far will this get you?" The multi-colored bill in his fingers would be more than enough. Without it, she couldn't afford to see him.

"Thank you." She tucked the bill into her pocket. Habit had her glancing around, her pulse kicking up. Being mugged and pick-pocketed more than once left a girl with a healthy dose of situational awareness.

"See ya, Daisy." He seemed to tear his gaze off her to smile at Ina. "And very nice to meet you, Mari."

Ina gave him a curt nod and started for the bus stop. Dalisay paused, but she had nothing to say. She just didn't want to go.

"Your mom's worried you'll be late." His voice had dropped low, intimate. It curled through her, leaving a warm tingle in her belly.

"Traffic," was all she said. Her mind was wiped out as she stared up at him. His short but unruly hair was so adorable that it prevented the rest of his masculinity from being intimidating.

And the rest of him was oh-so masculine.

"Dali!" Ina's voice cut through her thoughts.

Dalisay stiffened and then spun and jogged to Ina. She cast one last look over her shoulder.

Aaron waved, then tucked his hands into his pockets. People flowed around him as he watched them walk away. She peeled her gaze away before she veered into the street.

They walked in silence for a few moments.

"I like him," Dalisay finally said.

"I know."

They pressed together on the bus. Ina remained quiet. Dalisay's insides churned. They were in this together. As much as she liked Aaron, she couldn't run off with him and leave Ina to pay the consequences. Peejong would take her in, but she'd be miserable and utterly dependent on him and Sally.

"Tell me what you really think," Dalisay said.

Ina turned to her. "If he's the same guy we met, no duplicity, then…" She pressed her lips together and shook her head. "We don't have time for the getting-to-know-you period. He needs to marry you, or we're out on the streets."

The lease.

Ina continued. "Or I'm cleaning Peejong's home. And if Aaron won't marry you within a month, then we know who will. I'm telling you again: we're not bringing a man back to parade around the province who isn't committed to you."

Dalisay closed her eyes. No, that would be humiliating, and she already had one broken engagement.

Ina would accompany her for a few more dates, then she'd be on her own with Aaron and finally seal the deal. The slow burn of a developing relationship had to happen in days. They had their online time already. Now all she had to do was get him to say, "I do."

～

Aaron gazed out his hotel room window as he talked to Jackson. "Remind Mom your conference is tomorrow."

"I really don't care if she goes or not. I'm doing fine."

"She can still go and hear how well you're doing. And Nicolas?"

"Yeah, he's doing fine, too." Jackson's tone lightened in the way it does when he's protecting Nicolas and his floundering grades.

"Mom needs to go, and I want each of you to go with her."

"Dude, I'm a senior. I'm not trailing my mommy around the school."

"Dude, you're still in school." And Mom had to act like a mom every once in a while. "Is Dad there?"

"He's probably downstairs, asleep in front of the TV."

"Bring the phone to him so I can talk with him."

"Why?"

Aaron lifted his gaze to the ceiling. "Because he's doing my job for me while I'm gone, and I'd like to talk to him."

"You message like every day."

"Give him the damn phone."

"Fine," Jackson growled.

Nothing came over the other side but uneven breathing as his brother bounced down the stairs.

Dad's groggy voice came over the line. "What's up?"

"Did the haul yesterday go well?"

Dad grunted. He must be sitting up after having the recliner at full tilt. "Didn't do it."

Aaron rubbed his eyes. A week of turning his days and nights around, but the time difference still affected him. The stress over keeping track of four people's schedules half a world away didn't help. "Why?"

"Bad weather." Man of many words.

"Did you get the welding done on—"

"Aaron. It's been storming for two days. I can barely see the shop. Give it time. I'll get it done."

Aaron let out a sigh. Nicolas had mentioned a storm last time he called, and Aaron had been fresh off a date with Daisy—and her mom. They'd had him over to their apartment and stuffed him full of some of the best food—easy on the peppers. When Mom had cooked, her meals had come from a can or the freezer. Aaron could get spoiled with Mari's fresh food.

Daisy would arrive soon. He had to wrap this call up. "The boys have conferences. Can you remind Mom to go?"

"If she doesn't, I'll go."

"You won't be home in time if you're gonna haul."

"It'll be fine. Don't worry."

"The truck was in the shop during the storm?" It'd be a moody beast to start otherwise.

"Aaron, this isn't my first rodeo. How's Daisy? It sounds like everything is going well."

Dad hit on the one topic that could get Aaron's mind off farming. "We're having our first solo date."

"No mom to chaperone, eh? Now you two can really get to know each other, but I know you'll be a gentleman."

He didn't want to be a gentleman, that was for damn sure.

No, he did, but after a couple of months of talking and more talking, then being teased by the silky promise of her skin for days, his thoughts weren't honorable.

"Absolutely. She's going to be here in a few minutes. I'll talk to you later."

Dad cut the line first. Aaron stared at his screen. Should he call Mom about the conferences? She was probably asleep on the couch. Aaron doubted that she made the trek to their bedroom too often.

He shoved the phone into his pocket and plopped down onto the bed. The sheets were rumpled, the covers half thrown back. Daisy would ring the room from the lobby. If he thought she'd be up here, he would've straightened up.

Maybe he should anyway. Forget the room. Was he presentable? They'd made plans for a bay cruise at sunset. Chalk it up to the most romantic date he'd ever been on, and likely ever would be on. Unless he took Daisy on a lake cruise through the reeds at sunset in his fishing boat. That could be romantic, too.

Thinking of Daisy with him in Moore was…surreal. This was the closest he'd ever been to tying the knot. And he hadn't been alone with Daisy yet.

Yesterday, after lunch, Mari had looked at him and asked if he had the paperwork complete for the ceremony. Daisy had jumped in and the two women had argued back and forth in their language.

He needed to address the bull in the room with Daisy, but doing it around Mari was too awkward. It was clear the women were close. Daisy said it had been them against the world for several years, and they were fighting to stay in Manila over moving back home with the rest of their family. He didn't understand the problems with her relatives, but he knew family drama.

He propped his elbows on his knees and stared at his hands. The extent of how close he was with his parents and brothers hadn't been fully revealed. Jackson graduated at the end of the year and Nicolas the next year. Then he could ask his parents to move out.

But his brothers should have a stable place to come home to during their breaks. Could he live with feeling like he kicked his parents out? What would Daisy think of that? Would she think he was immature because they all resided under the same roof, or would she think he was a bastard for turning them out when they'd failed once on their own already?

Scrubbing his face, he sighed. Which had been better, being in the stasis of his life where no one wanted to spend it with him because of his living situation, or facing his living situation to finally get the chance to spend his life with someone?

Meeting Daisy wasn't a regret. She was quiet, unless her mother got her started. Then her eyes lit with fire and her face unveiled her emotions. But she wasn't meek, either. She spoke with confidence, without looking to Mari for approval or confirmation. Sweetness exuded from Daisy like it was her aura, but she wasn't innocent in a clueless way. She was in her twenties, had lost her father, moved from a tiny town to the big city on her own, and the irony of her letting her mom move in with her didn't escape him.

Mari had her shit together. His mother didn't.

The same old worries swelled up. Mom hadn't gotten better since they'd moved in. He and Dad had hoped that once the pressure of a mortgage and a full-time job was removed, she'd snap out of it and start giving a crap.

Mari gave a crap. And she let Daisy know it, but while it was obvious Daisy respected Mari, she didn't get run over by her. And she probably didn't have to remind her to go to work, pay her bills, or ask that she pick up a few groceries.

The room phone rang. He jumped to answer it, and the feminine voice on the other end seeped into his veins.

"Be right down, Daisy." He'd admit, he infused her name with a hint of suggestion. The longer he was around her, the harder it was not to.

Daisy. Mari called her Dali, but her name was as strong and guileless as she was. She'd told him Daisy was fine, and he got the impression it was the name he got to call her.

What would he tell his family to call her? They already called her Daisy. He feared he was Americanizing her name, but she'd assured him that many of their names overlapped with common American ones. *My name's actually Tagalog, after my dad's mom.* And she'd said her uncle's name was Peter John, but they all called him Peejong.

Before he popped out the door, he stopped in front of the full-length mirror attached to a closet door. Matching boots? Check. Combed hair? Still looked good. And he'd chosen a gray T-shirt with a mottled design that gave it a granite pattern. Not fancy by any means, but it'd work.

Down in the lobby, he found Daisy in their usual meeting spot. She hadn't seen him yet, and he slowed to enjoy the view.

Her head was turned as she stared out the eight foot glass doors. The entire front of the hotel was clear, the passersby clearly visible. The hotel was oriented farther away from the street than most of the eateries and stores he'd been in.

Upstairs, his suitcase was packed with souvenirs. Daisy helped him choose by asking pointed questions about his families' likes and dislikes so he wasn't just snatching and buying the first thing he could find.

When the price was given and he was about to hand over the money, Mari stepped in and got him the best deal possible. How much had she saved him?

Daisy's long hair was gathered over one shoulder. Sometimes she tied it back, but more often it hung unrestrained.

He couldn't tear his gaze off her legs. She'd worn slacks on their previous dates and favored her white set. He favored her white set, too. They wheeled his imagination into overdrive.

In her black dress that hit a few inches above her knees, she proved that his fantasies were not unrealistic. Her smooth legs had as many curves as her body and his fingers itched to trace along them, to savor the heat of her skin.

The flare of her hips was covered by a sleeveless jacket that was fancier than a vest. But he knew the shape of her body by heart, was familiar with the sway of her hips when she was both meandering along and speed walking to keep up with Mari.

As if sensing the lick of his gaze on her, she turned toward him. Her face brightened, and a hint of pink tinged her cheeks.

Was he grinning like a boy with his first tractor? That moment when he got to drive it all by himself and learn the real idiosyncrasies of the machine?

Hell, had he just compared Daisy to a tractor?

He crossed to her. "You look amazing." Leaning down, he brushed a kiss over her cheek. It was all he'd managed to gut out in front of her mother. Only this time he landed closer to her mouth. Her blush had deepened, and as he pulled away, her gaze touched his lips.

"Thank you," she murmured. "You do, too."

He clasped her hand, another move he'd been too chickenshit to do the last three times because her mother had been around. They walked outside together. They were going to eat before calling a taxi to take them to the dock. "I don't look like I just rolled out of bed, so that's an improvement."

She squeezed his hand. "But I like that look on you, too."

The warm glow that sparked regressed him a good fifteen years to the first time a girl said she thought he was hot. "Just remember that when I'm covered in dust and smell like exhaust."

The change in her was instantaneous. Her hand only rested in his and her shoulders sagged. The look on her face worried him. Serious, almost grim.

"Is that a deal breaker?" he asked, half joking. He'd been serious. His job got him dirty and with so much going on at home, aesthetics weren't his priority.

She stopped and put her hand on his chest. Without

thinking, he clasped his hand over it. They stood in the middle of the sidewalk like that, almost embracing.

"Of course not," she clarified. "But tonight, we need to talk about us and what's going to happen and when."

He ducked his head. "I agree. You're the one moving across the world. You need to prepare." He wasn't going anywhere. Each day was a struggle to stay away from the farm and the magnitude of work that needed to be done. Winter was their slow season, but no time of the year was easy with his brothers and parents to look after.

He put himself in Daisy's place; there was no comparison. She was upending her life, leaving her only family, to live with him.

She stared straight ahead, her gaze on his chest. He thought he'd feel like he towered over her, but her personality didn't allow it. The sure way she carried herself, the strength in her quiet voice, put her on an equal level with him. Whatever she said, he'd do. Sit. Stay. Beg.

"It's not just that." Her fingers curled into the material of his shirt. "I'll explain it all, and I hope... I hope you're not... I hope we're okay. I like you."

"I like you, too," he said gruffly. "A lot. If it weren't for you, I'd have turned back home in a second."

Her expression turned crestfallen. Shit. He'd just insulted her home.

"No, it's not here. I mean, it's different here, but not in a bad way. You've made me into shrimp's number one fan. But I'm gone from my job and a lot of people count on me. It's hard to run things this far away, even with technology."

Understanding dawned, followed by relief. "I didn't think about that. I'm sorry."

He lifted his hand off hers to caress her face. Until they started moving again, he didn't want to quit touching her. If he was at home, and she was any other girl, he'd ask them to chuck their boating plans out the window and have raw, needy sex—not in those exact words—but this was his future wife. She needed to know that there was more between them than a contract and a bed. *He* needed her to know.

"There's nothing to be sorry for. I've never been this far from home and never for this long. It's been hard, but I'll be back soon."

She blinked and withdrew her fingers from his chest. Their other hands were still clasped, and she towed him along.

Had he said something again?

They walked for blocks, and she described the restaurant they were going to. Fancier than the previous ones he'd eaten at, but within walking distance.

Once they were seated and their food ordered, he broached the subject. "About us. We started this thing with the intention to get married, and now we're here. I feel like I need to propose or something." His eyes flew wide. He had no ring!

Her brows lifted. He must looked panicked.

"I didn't think of buying an engagement ring," he clarified.

"Maybe we can pick them out together." She snapped her mouth closed like she'd said too much.

"I'd love that. I don't want to get anything you'd hate." He dragged in a deep breath and sat back. "So we're doing this, huh?"

Her blush returned. "Yes. My family in the province will be thrilled to celebrate a wedding. We can contract the marriage here in Manila and marry when we reach the province."

Marry in the province. Like, this week? "Get married now?" His voice squeaked.

"Wasn't that what you meant?"

"I thought…" He shook his head. "If we married here, you still wouldn't be able to come home with me. And I can't stay. It'll take months for your visa to clear and…I just can't stay."

"I will wait here, but…"

"I can't marry you before any of my family has met you." They'd all think they were right. That he'd rushed to buy a wife. That she was after him for something other than love. "I live in a small town. If I showed up married with no wife after a trip overseas, they'd think—"

"They'd think you mail ordered a bride," she said matter-of-factly.

"Yes. I don't want that for you." He didn't want her walking around town, earning looks of pity because she'd had to marry the crazy Walker boy. Those in Moore familiar with his family, which was most everyone, thought highly of his cousins, but not as highly of him. His cousins had all met women, gotten married, started families, and he cruised around town getting critiqued on his appearance and dumped by his dates.

She exhaled and looked around the restaurant. He ignored the six-foot aquariums along the wall and the tinkling of the water in the fountain placed in the middle of the seating area. The fluorescent lights bounced off her dark hair and glimmered in the depths of her deep brown eyes.

"Daisy?"

She lifted her gaze to him.

"What's wrong?"

"Ina doesn't want to bring you to meet the family if we aren't committed. And I agree with her. Just like your small town, the gossip of us will spread like monsoon rains."

"Will it help to buy the rings beforehand?"

Her eyes flared with approval, then dimmed again.

He had to reassure her that he wasn't here to mess with her emotions for his own sick needs. Like her, he was serious about forever. "I honestly hadn't thought about marrying here. I thought we'd meet, then I'd go home and file the visa paperwork and we'd marry when it cleared." He lifted a shoulder. "And my family would be present, but I don't want to demand that when you can't have it."

A smile lifted one side of her mouth and she fiddled with her napkin. "Bringing you to meet them all will be enough."

Her eyes were pensive, and she twisted the cloth napkin.

"Then what else is wrong?"

With a heavy sigh, she dropped the napkin and gave the clown fish in the aquarium one last look, as if she were seeking confirmation to tell him. "The idea to look for an American husband was mine, but we both made the decision because we can't afford to keep living the way we are. My lease is up at the end of the month and if I were to sign a new one, it'd include a rent increase I can't cover."

"And you'd have to move back to the province?" His curiosity grew to visit the place she'd grown up. Why didn't she want to go back?

"I would. And I'd be pressured to settle with a friend of the family. He's a nice guy, but we went to school together and there's no chemistry." She glanced away and muttered, "And his family is more overbearing than mine."

Beads of jealously and irritation dripped into his blood. Her relatives had someone else picked out for her, and she wouldn't have a say because she'd be beholden to them? Daisy's self-assuredness seemed to stop at her family. "Is there nowhere else in Manila that you can afford?"

She shook her head, her eyes downcast. "If it were just me, perhaps. But a two bedroom costs more and then there's the cost of moving and leasing a new place."

If they got married at the end of the week, she could stay with her family as a married woman even if he flew home.

But then she'd come to Moore with opinions already formed about her. It wasn't exactly a win-win for her.

"Would they let you stay with them if you were engaged to me?"

She considered his question. "Yes. We'd all be living in the same house, but for only a little time it won't be so bad. Ina would get a job as a live-in housekeeper, and I could stay and help around his house until I could fly to the US."

Would she still be encouraged to start something with this other guy? Daisy would be alone, without her mom, without him, but have this man who must've at least agreed to consider marrying her.

If he'd grown up with her then he'd know how sexy she was, probably want her as much as Aaron did.

Wait—she'd said they'd all be living together. And she hadn't sounded thrilled. *Only a little time it won't be so bad.*

He hadn't been clear about how close his parents and brothers lived. He should say something. But later.

There was another option that worked for her and would settle his guilt about his lack of clarity. He had to give himself a few seconds to ponder it. The first girl he'd "bumped" online hadn't made him completely jaded, but he couldn't be a sucker. Daisy didn't make him feel like a fool who'd fall for an easy line though. "I can pay for a room for you until the visa clears."

Her mouth opened, she shut it and frowned. "You'd do that?"

"Of course. You shouldn't have to be terribly inconvenienced because I want to marry in my hometown."

"And Ina? She'll look for a job as soon as we confirm our plans, but…"

"Not an issue."

Her smile was so big, it was hard not to drag her next to him and curl her slight body into his. He wanted nothing more than a kiss, but they were seated on opposite sides of the booth. Too formal.

Their food arrived at that moment. When their server disappeared, he gently slid her plate of oysters next to his and scooted over in his seat.

He cocked his head to invite her over.

Her eyes heated, and she spun around the table next to him.

"That's better," he said.

"Yes." She gazed up at him. "It is."

# CHAPTER 9

The solid warmth of Aaron's body intoxicated her. The boat cruise was almost over, and she was burrowed into his side. The longer they were together, the more they touched and cuddled. The sun had gone down; only lingering rays of oranges and reds were left in the sky. The boat had gone far enough out that Manila's air pollution didn't hinder the view.

After their conversation in the restaurant, he'd set a time to go pick out engagement rings.

Wearing an engagement ring wasn't necessary, but it would be a solid symbol to show around the province. And something from Aaron to hold onto when he went back home.

Her heart hung heavy. She'd seen him every day since he arrived. He was her first thought when she woke and her last before she closed her eyes. Financial struggles and the loss of her dad had dominated her thoughts for so long, it was a refreshing change. But he'd be a bittersweet thought while he was gone.

The announcement was made that they'd be pulling in to disembark soon.

She sat up to stretch her back. Aaron's arm curled around her waist and tugged her closer.

"We should do this again before we go," he murmured into her ear, his deep voice sending shivers down her spine.

She turned her face up to tell him that she'd love to. He lowered his head and paused a breath above her lips.

Her breath suspended in her lungs. Their first kiss. She was starting to think this day wouldn't come. He'd been shy in front of Ina, and she hadn't blamed him.

Heat infused his eyes, deepening the blue. Her breath hitched. Was he going to kiss her, or was this far as they were going to get? It was a merciless tease.

Her heart rate kicked up, and her gaze dipped to his mouth. Those lips she had wondered about for days. Was he a soft kisser? Demanding? Would he be hesitant, leaving the kiss at barely more than a peck?

There was a lot of expectation of the first kiss for a couple who'd already talked about marriage.

Finally, his warm lips pressed to hers. She swayed farther into him, her hand clutching at his shirt.

This was the best first kiss ever. Firm, but gentle, he held her in his embrace the same way he kissed. They were their own island on the boat, the din of conversation fading until there was nothing but learning the taste and feel of Aaron.

He tightened his arms until she was as smashed into him as she could be. This thing could work between them. Her crazy idea of looking for an American man to marry didn't seem so impulsive and reckless when she was in the arms of a man like Aaron.

Every inch of his body that she was pressed against was hard. He was a fit man and probably looked as good without clothes as he did with them on.

Oh…her mind was going there. Aaron and her naked. But as he claimed her, their tongues twining, thinking about them going farther physically wasn't a stretch. She wanted to marry a man she had chemistry with, a man she could fall in love with. And this kiss made it seem like that was within her grasp.

His groan rumbled into her, and he deepened the kiss.

*Yes, please.*

Her heart thudded, warmth pooling in her belly until it was all she could do not to climb into his lap and straddle him in the middle of the crowd. Heat ignited a demanding ache between her thighs. When was the last time she'd felt like this?

The gin pom pi they'd had on the cruise flavored his kiss. It'd go down as her most favorite drink in the world.

She was engaged. Getting the air kissed out of her by a man she could be crazy about. Probably safe to say *was* crazy about. But she could fall in love with him. Desperately easy, was probably halfway there when her sensible side wasn't whispering in her ear that she still had to move across the world and meet the real Aaron Walker.

Her ex had taught her not to be foolish again. Both she and Ina had gone into this matchmaking affair carefully, fully aware, and it'd be a letdown to herself and her mother if she naively handed her heart to Aaron.

But she'd enjoy the rest of his visit.

His embrace softened, a signal this was coming to end. She didn't want it to, but she also didn't want to be a spectacle, and if it continued any longer, they would be.

The smolder in his gaze wasn't concealed as he glanced around. A brow arched at someone over her shoulder. The heat in his gaze dimmed to a stare of warning.

"Someone watching us?" she whispered. Hard muscle tensed under the hand she rested on his chest, and it was all she could do not to stroke him in public. Her body pled for more, but she had to cool her physical reaction before she made a scene.

Aaron was staring at someone, and he held his warning glare a moment longer before he spoke low in her ear. "A kid was going to take a picture of us. I think I busted him in time before he put us up on InstaChat or Snapgram or whatever they're called."

She laid her head on his chest as the boat bumped and swayed against the dock. The trip was ending and she'd almost forgotten, but Aaron must've been aware enough or they would've been making out as the passengers departed.

A grin tickled her lips. Look at her. The last few years, she'd been feeling a good couple of decades older than she was, had felt like her dreams for a career in nursing and a man to spend her life with were gone. But here she was, not caring if a hundred photos were snapped of her and Aaron, or if they'd have to be pried apart once the tour was done.

Her dream to finish school had crept back into her mind. The last few evenings after work, she'd jumped on and checked out the requirements for nursing school. If her basics transferred, she wouldn't need many more credits before she could apply. Aaron had said Moore had a small hospital and a few nursing homes. She could get her foot in the door at one as an aide to gain some experience to help her get accepted.

Excitement built the more she thought about it. All aspirations, thoughts, and fantasies had been wiped from her mind when she'd had to withdraw from university. If she didn't allow herself to think about it, then it couldn't depress her, or make Ina feel responsible in any way.

Their night had come to an end. Aaron rose, bringing her with him. They wrapped their arms around each other as they wound through the dock and back to the spot where they would wait for their taxi.

"I've been spoiled driving everywhere," he mused.

"Do you miss it?"

"Yeah, actually. To come and go as I please. My truck is like a second office, but more than that, it's a necessity, a way of life. I live too far out of town to walk. Once I'm in town, I doubt the bus…" His face screwed up. "I don't even know if Moore has a bus other than the senior center transport bus. Anyway, businesses are spread out. You don't have a grocery store on one end of the block and the hardware store on the other. They're at opposite ends of town. Downtown, businesses are close together, but then half the year isn't amenable to walking."

"The weather is that bad? Or people just aren't used to it?"

He smiled, shadows playing over his face. The ridges of his jaw and cheekbones stood out, and she pressed a hand to her fluttering belly. Aaron was a good-looking man. And she was going to marry him.

"Both, I guess. I don't know that anyone could get used to walking in twenty-below zero weather, but I'm sure it can be done."

"Do you have taxis?"

He blinked. "Maybe? I've never needed one."

A curl of unease rolled through her. Little choice for public transportation. No walking. How would she get from his house—their house—to school? Or work? How would she leave to do…anything?

"Did I say something wrong?" he asked.

She smothered her dismay but had to inquire further. Be sensible. "I'm wondering how I'd get around."

"We'd get you a car. And your license once you get settled."

The way he said it made it sound easy. She hadn't known him long, but she trusted him about this. A good sign.

Their ride arrived, and he made sure she was buckled before him. His knuckles turned white as he gripped the seat on the trip to her apartment.

He caught her looking. "I swear I'll never get used to this kind of driving. I feel like we're on the Indy 500." At her questioning look. "Car racing."

Would he feel better if he were the one driving? He struggled each time they caught a cab, though he tried not to show it, and he'd mentioned how hard it was being away from his work. Was he the kind who needed control?

Did it matter? As long as he wasn't dictating what she could and couldn't do, well… She grabbed his hand. No, she was being paranoid. He'd shown none of those signs, nor the nearly unperceivable tendency to dictate her life like her uncle. Even if he did, again, did it matter? It was either Peejong or Aaron, and she had hopes for a life of her own choosing with Aaron, as ironic as it seemed—meeting a man to marry online.

On the way back, she and Aaron held hands but remained quiet. Ina had moved so soon after her father's death, and Dalisay had understood, having lived around Peejong and Sally all her life. But now it was crystal clear. The relationship her parents had was what she wanted. A relationship full of love and respect, both parties working hard to please the other and build a good life together.

No wonder Ina hadn't been interested in finding her own love connection online. *I'm not what those men are looking for,* she'd scoff. She'd had her dream once. Why risk tarnishing it with a false marriage?

The car slammed to a stop in front of her building. She asked the driver to wait as she clambered out with Aaron. He towered over her. Not in an intimidating way, but in a way she welcomed. His presence, the heat of his body, the smell of his soap, and the open water scent of their cruise clung to him.

"Tomorrow then?" His gaze simmered with desire. Hers must be identical. "We'll pick out rings."

"Tomorrow." A few more days and they'd be together for the trip to visit her relatives. She wouldn't have him alone, but they'd be together.

Heat infused his eyes, deepening the blue. He dipped his head and caught her mouth. She curved into him, the reaction natural. His lips were soft but firm, and she responded like she'd been made for him.

Wrapping her arms around his neck, she tugged him closer. There was no hesitancy this time, no cautious testing of the waters. They both wanted more than a kiss, but this was all they'd be allowed, at least until they returned from visiting family. After that, they'd have a couple more nights like this before he had to return home.

The ache in her belly returned full force until she ground against him to seek relief. He tightened his grip until she rocked against him to assuage the sweet throb between her legs. Oh god, she never acted like this. But this man was hers.

They were getting married. And she was losing her mind over his kisses. Just imagining what else there was left her body feeling heavy and needy.

He answered her desire by cupping her butt and clutching her to him. She could climb him and wrap her legs around him so easily. The idea sounded better and better. The length of him hardening between them would be centered just right and—

The cab honked, but Aaron didn't break apart. He lingered over her mouth, caressing her tongue with his. Her hands were buried in his hair and she was on her tiptoes.

At the second honk, she pulled away, missing the press of his body immediately. "Tomorrow," was all she could say.

He nodded and stiffly bent into the back of the cab. A smile played over her lips. This was officially the best date ever.

When the taillights of the taxi faded, she jogged upstairs. She burst into her apartment with a giant grin. Ina was at the table. Dalisay had asked her not to wait up for her, but they both had known she would.

Ina lifted her gaze from the book she read. Her face was a mask of calm, but Dalisay sensed the burn of the ultimate question.

She quenched Ina's curiosity. "I need to message Richard and tell him that I'm no longer available."

Ina closed her eyes briefly. It wasn't the jubilant whoop Dalisay had hoped for, more like the look of a mother whose worry was never over. But when she opened her eyes, she grinned in return.

For the hundredth time, Aaron's gaze strayed to Dalisay's left finger, decorated with the engagement ring they'd picked out.

He was an engaged man.

The bus cruised along. He, Daisy, and Mari had arranged for a ride to the provincial town she was from. The city was out of view behind him, swallowed up by lush green land. The longer they traveled, the more rugged and rural the land grew. Palm trees and fronds sprouted from the land. The swell of mountains lined the horizon.

His arm was slung around Daisy, and her mom sat on the other side of the aisle.

Daisy and her mom explained everything he was passing.

The city was fascinating, but as a country kid, the rural land was far more intriguing to him. He made out farmland, the familiar outline of a field as recognizable as an emergency flare. According to Daisy, they grew corn and rice and a variety of smaller crops around Solano.

They'd stopped in small towns for a rest and to exchange passengers. So not like Manila. So not like Moore, either, but he could pick out similarities. Local businesses, residents who knew each other's personal stories. He doubted a small town anywhere in the world lacked a gossip mill.

Each stop, he'd get out and stretch, walk around, and mainly, check his phone.

Right before Daisy rang him to say she and Mari had arrived at the hotel, he'd called to tell his family the news that he was officially engaged. They both had chosen their rings, and he'd kept it until after they ate when he proposed properly. Different from his expectations, but so was Daisy.

After Dad's "hey, that's great," Aaron had asked about the farm. The cold spell after the winter storm had knocked out Mom's car battery. The temperatures dropped enough today to turn the rain to ice, and the power was flickering. Dillon had called Dad and said his house was out of power. Topping off the gas to the generators hadn't been on his to-do list before Aaron left, so Dad planned to brave the roads in the morning to grab supplies—of all fuel types…because Jackson had missed the grocery run and Mom hadn't left the house all week. So they were out of food.

Motherfucker.

He pulled out his phone again. By the time Dad got up and crawled his way to town on the black ice that no doubt lined the highway, Aaron would be hit and miss with cell coverage. Daisy said her hometown had decent service, but he had no idea if it was the same he used.

No messages. No missed calls.

Daisy patted his leg. "Still no word?"

"Nope." Why'd it have to storm while he was gone? Some Novembers passed with mild weather and barely any precipitation. Other Novembers gave a whopping preview to what it was like to suffer winter in the Midwest.

His skin crawled to get home. His mind clicked through the list of things to take care of. Shit. He could've reminded Dad or messaged his brothers to check with Travis for extra fuel. Maybe only one side of the road that stretched through his and his cousins' property was out of power and they could spare fuel—and food. Brock probably had an extra battery on hand. Would Dad think of checking with him? To Dad, Brock was still the quiet kid that was hard to talk to.

He tucked his phone away and scrubbed his face. Having Daisy next to him whisked some of his angst away, but if he could fly home tomorrow, he would.

"We'll be at Solano in two more hours and you can try to call before we leave for Peejong's." She sounded as optimistic as he felt. They'd get a taxi to her uncle's and spend two nights at her uncle's and head back on the third day. He'd call as soon as Manila was in sight.

He'd been away from home too long.

The rest of the trip passed with Daisy dozing on him and a thousand items he wanted to tend to at home running through his head. Mari chatted to the woman next to her.

She'd been friendlier with him since the engagement. The spring in her step was like a giant weight had been shoved off her shoulders. Daisy would miss her terribly.

They'd have to come visit.

He sighed. More time away. He could prepare better. Buy in bulk so his parents wouldn't have to worry about stocking for bad weather. Dammit, did Dad have a winter survival kit in his truck? He'd probably gotten rid of it when he'd moved to town.

They approached a smattering of buildings. Without the haze of the city, the view all around him was crisper than any picture online he'd scanned through. Would it be like this for Daisy when she came to Minnesota? She'd said she'd combed through pictures, but when it came to nature's beauty, pictures didn't always do it justice.

Solano was bigger than Moore but had the feel of a small town. Like his hometown, buildings weren't built tall, but flat. The architecture was unlike anything found in Moore. Ornate, but not in an overly ostentatious way. They passed churches, schools, grocery stores, and shops.

"You grew up here?"

"Yes." Her wistful tone matched her expression. "I really did like it here. But I got into a good university in Manila and hoped the city would have more job opportunities."

She'd been in a nursing program, but she never talked about it other than mentioning she'd like to look at finishing her degree.

"Why didn't you stay in the healthcare field after you left school? Couldn't you have been an aide or something?"

Her smile was sad. "Probably, but I wanted a clean break. If I couldn't finish, then I didn't want any part of it." She nudged him. "And I don't get tips in the hospital."

He chuckled. "Probably a good thing. I get it, though. If I had to move off the farm, I don't think I'd want anything to do with it. It'd be hard to get away from farming in Moore. If I sold cars, I'd have farmers and ranchers asking about trucks up for the job. If I sold insurance, there'd be crop insurance. I'd see people I know from the industry all over town."

Frowning, his dad came to mind. Was that Dad's problem? He missed it? But then why'd he retire? No, there had to be another reason Dad had grappled with town life. And a reason why Mom wrestled with town *and* country life.

Daisy squeezed his hand. "I can get away from medical

life easier. We toured the hospital in town when I was in high school and I was hooked. As a kid, I was always the one asking Ina how everything with our body worked and running to get bandages for my friends." She shot him a sly grin. "I may have over-bandaged them."

He dropped a kiss on her head. "I bet they had the best care."

Her expression grew solemn the farther into town they got. "It's weird being back here."

"Haven't been back since your dad died?"

She shook her head, sorrow in her eyes. "When Ina moved in with me, she took care of everything and left."

He lowered his voice. "She was that determined not to move in with her brother?"

Daisy snorted and muttered, "Ina would've walked to Manila before that happened."

"Can't wait to meet him." He gave her a wink.

He was as prepared as he could be for facing her over-bearing relatives. The parents of his previous dates had been congenial enough, but always with the undercurrent of over-protectiveness. Daisy's family wouldn't be hostile. Shouldn't be hostile. He could handle it.

They reached the bus stop. He shuttled Daisy and Mari off and grabbed their luggage. They both packed lighter than he had and shared a suitcase. He looked high maintenance compared to them.

Bustling out of the way of the small crowd, he retrieved his phone. "Mind if I call home while you arrange a ride?"

Daisy nodded and went in search of a taxi, Mari following her.

He checked the time. It'd be in the middle of the night, but he had to try. Peejong lived outside of Solano and might have a signal booster, but Aaron didn't want the anxiety of his family without power to overshadow the visit.

"Aaron?" Dad answered groggily. "Everything okay?"

"That's what I called to ask you. Our last conversation had me worried."

Dad groaned like he was stretching. "I got the generator going just in time for the power to turn back on."

"But you made it to town and back fine?"

"Yep. At least it wasn't a wasted trip. They're forecasting a bigger storm late next week. Hope it doesn't affect your flight."

"What?"

Dad chuckled. "It'll be a Thanksgiving to remember, that's for sure."

"How much snow?" His flight might be delayed. Dammit. He was chomping to get back and jump in to pick up the slack he left behind.

"They're saying a foot, but you know how it goes. We won't know until closer to the time. So have you met the family yet?"

"We're on our way." *I couldn't relax until I knew you all were alive and not freezing fingers and toes off.*

"Then go and have fun. Don't worry about us. We know the drill."

*Then why were you so unprepared?* "Did Mom make it to conferences?"

The silence on the other end said it all. "She wasn't feeling well, you know..."

Aaron hung his head. She had one job. "Yeah. I know." He lifted his head and forced a sigh down. Daisy waved at him from a kiosk. "Hey, I'll call again as soon as I can."

He disconnected, but the conversation plowed through his mind. Another storm when he was supposed to return home. What if he got stranded in Minneapolis because Moore's tiny airport couldn't get a plane in during bad weather? A night or two in the cities wouldn't hurt, but he'd be gone and unable to help during another whopper of a storm.

Stuffing his phone away, he adjusted his shoulders and rotated his neck to relax. Daisy didn't need to see him upset. He crossed to them.

"Got us a ride?" he asked when he reached them.

She nodded. "We asked for it right away. Peejong will have a feast ready for us when we get there."

"I bet he's excited to see you both."

"Oh yes," Mari said. Her jaw was tight, and she was scanning the street like Peejong was going to jump out of the bushes.

She and her sister-in-law must really be on the outs.

Daisy laid a hand on her mom's arm. "Peejong will at least. Sally maybe not."

Mari harrumphed, but inclined her head.

Daisy glanced at him. "She assured me they're always civil, but she hates feeling the judgment."

"Yeah, I can get that." He wasn't in the same boat as Mari when he walked around Moore. No one person gave him a hard time. It slipped into conversations and he heard about it from his friends and relatives.

Maybe it wouldn't burn so badly if half the gossip weren't true.

The Jeepney pulled up. He and the driver loaded the bags and they all hopped in. For two short days, he would cast his frustrations aside and marinate in getting to know Daisy through her family. Once they were heading back to Manila, he'd plan his trip back to Moore.

# CHAPTER 10

Dalisay listened as Aaron rambled his plan off to her. Her heart sank more with each detail he shared. She slowed her walk, and he adjusted his pace until they were facing each other. The path around Peejong's property was cleared of branches, and her cousins used it enough that the undergrowth had worn away to a dirt trail. It'd rained a few days ago, but it was dry enough to walk on without getting her shoes or Aaron's boots muddy.

They had arrived the previous evening to a large gathering and a spread of food that stuffed them all. Roasted pig and chicken, rice, and peppers, along with her aunt's renowned coconut milk pudding.

Aaron had sampled everything, even the peppers, which he ruefully regretted.

As he talked, he lifted his hat and wiped his brow. The day was warm, but he'd muttered about the humidity only once. They'd walked about half of a mile from Peejong's house while she showed him the chicken coops and the rice fields. Her uncle even had a few banana trees and several palm trees they harvested coconuts from.

His hair stuck to his head. He towered over her, standing so he blocked the sun. Always considerate.

Except for what he was telling her. Well, he was being thoughtful explaining it all, but it was tearing her up inside.

"So I'll change my flight to fly out the day after we get back instead of a week after." He stopped and gauged her reaction. "I'm really sorry," he said quietly, feathering a finger along her cheek.

She turned her face into his touch, wanting so much more. "I understand. The day was coming where you'd have to leave, but I didn't think it'd be so disappointing."

"That's a good thing then." His voice had grown husky. Had she moved closer, or had he?

"I want to spend as much time with you as I can. I'll call in sick the night before you leave, and we can spend the evening together."

Hope flared in his eyes. "I don't want you to get in trouble."

She shrugged. "I never miss work. One night won't hurt."

He skimmed his hand down her neck. For such a warm day, his hot touch should be uncomfortable, but she'd welcome the blanket of his body. Neediness uncoiled in her belly. When was the last time she'd felt like this? With her ex? Sort of. Before? Not really.

She spread her hands on his chest. The rise and fall was steady, like his touch. His gaze dipped to her left hand.

"I can't tell you what seeing that ring on your finger does to me." The rumble of his words vibrated through her center, pooling between her legs.

"I know exactly what it does."

His eyes widened, the stark appreciation written across his face. She glided her hands up his shoulders and buried them in his short hair. She tugged him down to her and he came, slowly, like he was savoring the wait.

Their lips touched for a moment, then parted, and they met each other's gaze. Heat vibrated between them. Things were going to change. As if it wasn't real before, it was now. It'd only been superficial before. The getting-to-know-you stage.

And, oh, she wanted to know him. Her eyelids drifted shut as he closed the distance between them again. A soft touch at first, before the spark between them ignited into a raging fire. She opened and invited him in. Their kiss deepened until she didn't know where she stopped and he began. The buildup between them had come to this.

They'd had to be good for too long. Her family had dominated his time, asking him about Minnesota, the weather, his family. They were genuinely interested and not just ignoring Ina. In fact, Aaron's presence seemed to deflate the tension Dalisay had expected. That probably won Ina over more than anything else Aaron could've done. Her family spoke English as much as possible and Aaron had no problems understanding.

When Peejong learned Aaron farmed, then there was nothing Dalisay could say to stop the interrogation. Aaron pulled out his phone and scrolled through pictures of massive tractors and trucks. Peejong did the same, but much of his equipment was on a smaller scale. Peejong employed several people. They must've been bent over the screens for two hours talking about their farms.

But now he was all hers. A low growl escaped from him; she answered with a whimper.

She'd had zero clue that when she'd logged onto a dating site that it could turn out this well.

His hands roamed up and down her back. God help her, she rubbed against him. Anything to ease the ache in her belly only one thing could cure. Both of them naked and alone.

It couldn't happen now, but she'd get as much in as she could.

He cupped her butt, tightened his hold, released, and skirted a hand up her side as if to cup a breast. He stopped short.

She pulled away from him long enough to whisper, "Yes."

He grinned, captured her mouth again, and licked inside. She opened, greedy for him. Arching her back as much as she could without breaking their smoldering kiss, she gave him the access he needed.

His large hand scooped under her breast, his finger and thumb seeking her nipple through the thin material of her shirt.

A moan escaped. If it felt this good with clothes on, how would his work-roughened hand feel when they finally had sex?

She wanted to find out. Desperately.

Wrapping her arms around his broad shoulders wasn't possible without losing the ecstasy he was promising, so she gripped his biceps.

Rock hard.

The man worked for a living.

She rocked her pelvis. It wasn't enough. She tilted her hips again. He answered with the same motion.

Their tongues twined; their breaths mingled. He switched hands, giving much needed attention to her other nipple.

He released her mouth to moan her name.

They undulated against each other. With their height difference, she was safely ensconced in the protection of his body. She rested her head on his chest, smashing his arm between them, her body bowed to rock against him.

He kissed her head, nibbled down to her ear. His hot breath wafted over her sensitive flesh and almost pushed her over the edge.

"Da-li!" a young kid's voice called.

She pulled back with a gasp. Peejong's youngest, her little pal, Mark Rio, was looking for her.

Aaron craned to look over his shoulder. "I don't think he can see us."

No. And she wasn't in a state of undress. Neither was Aaron. Although…the impressive bulge in his jeans would give anyone who'd gone through puberty an indication of what was going on.

He followed her gaze. His smile was sheepish but also full of promise. "We need to walk back slowly so I can get myself under control."

She trailed a finger along his arm. "Are you saying I make you lose control?"

"You make me wanna." He grinned. His blue eyes sparkled like the river behind them. Taking a breath, he threw his shoulders back and spun them to face the trail back home. "On our leisurely stroll back, you can tell me about the birds I hear. They aren't the subtle songs of ours back home."

"Dali!" Mark Rio drew closer, but she still couldn't see him. At eight, he wouldn't give up. The look of utter adoration he gave Aaron wouldn't let him.

"We're coming," she called.

Mark Rio started to shout something when a shriek rang out.

Dalisay didn't wait to spare a look at Aaron. She took off, Aaron close behind her. Within seconds of flying down the path, Mark Rio came into view. He was sprawled on the ground with his bicycle still between his legs, the back wheel spinning.

He was crying and trying to move out from under the bike. Each time he gained an inch, he'd let out a holler.

Blood ran down his leg.

"Wait," she ordered.

He went still, but each time he peeked at his calf, he whimpered. The bike pedal had lacerated his little leg, and the cut was bleeding freely.

She tried to rip at her shirt for material to press against the wound. Aaron saw what she was doing and yanked off his shirt. Buttons flew in all directions before it was tossed at her. She caught it and dropped to her knees by Mark Rio.

Murmuring encouraging words to him, she motioned to Aaron to move the bike. With the bike out of the way, she tied the shirt around Mark Rio's lower leg. As she held pressure against it, she raised it in the air.

"Aaron, can you carry him back? I'll take the bicycle."

"Absolutely." He hefted Mark Rio, and she adjusted the boy so his leg wasn't hanging. Snapping the bicycle up, they trotted back to Peejong's.

Ina popped out of the house first, like she'd been on the lookout, having been left at the mercy of Sally. Ina called for Sally and ran toward them.

Mark Rio was handed off. Dalisay stayed by his side to tend to the injury. The bleeding slowed and once it was washed, it wasn't as bad as initially thought. She reassured the family and helped Sally securely bandage it. When he was finally resting, Dalisay left him in his mother's care and went in search of Aaron.

He was outside of the house with Mark Rio's teenage brother. They were standing by the chicken coop. Aaron had put on a clean shirt.

She'd missed him shirtless, so intent on her patient that she couldn't remember registering that Aaron had been bare chested.

Her patient. Dare she get her hopes up?

When he spotted her, he started over. "How is the little man?"

"Resting."

"Good." A slow grin formed. "Want to go for another walk?"

Tucking herself back under his arm, they walked back down the same trail they'd come from, and she planned his last night in Manila.

~

AARON TOSSED the last article of clothing into his suitcase. Add the last of his toiletries in the morning and he was ready for the long flight home.

A smaller part of him than he'd expected wanted to go home. Back to his bed. Which wasn't as plush as this one. Back to his truck. It'd be nice to drive where he wanted to go again. Back to the food he was used to. He'd adapted well. In the first few days, he'd sampled enough to know what he liked and what he should stay away from. He missed his steak and potatoes, but it was winter, and he didn't grill in the frigid temps anyway.

Daisy was arriving soon. To his room. To spend the night.

He rubbed the back of his neck as if it'd stave off the stirring in his manhood. It'd been hard enough to control his body's reaction to her while they were around her family, then sitting beside her for another six hours on the bus ride back to Manila.

A box of condoms rested in the drawer of the end table. He'd been almost ashamed of himself for packing them. How could things go so far without him feeling like he was taking advantage of the woman he'd met online?

But they had. And Daisy had asked to sleep over. He should've been the bigger person and planned to cuddle her all night, but the truth was, he'd waited his whole life for a woman like her. He didn't want to waste one more second. Add in the months they'd be apart waiting for her visa and his early trip home to his hot mess of a family, and it felt right to spend tonight together.

Spend the night. His mouth went dry. He surveyed the room. The bed was made, and no clothes hung off chairs or were strewn across the floor. He'd have to make more of an effort to keep his house looking this neat.

There was a soft knock at the door.

His breath hitched, and he stared at it. With a quick shake of his head, he jumped to answer.

Daisy waited for him, wearing the same black dress she wore on their boat trip. Her long hair begged for him to run his hands through it. The tint of flush in her cheeks, and the way her eyes licked over his body, made him more certain about tonight.

"Come on in. Hungry?"

"Not yet," she said breathlessly.

"Me, either." The click of the door shutting echoed in the room.

"Daisy—"

"Aaron—" She giggled. "You go."

"I don't really know what I was going to say. Besides that I think your name is beautiful. Dalisay." Her family called her Dali, and whenever she'd had to give her name, she used Dalisay.

Her serene smile cut through his nerves. "But I like when you call me Daisy."

The waiting was over. He pulled her close. Starting at her forehead, he trailed kisses to her mouth.

She didn't hesitate. While they were in their lip lock, she fisted his shirt and yanked it out of his pants.

Okay then.

He let her set the pace. She drew away from him to eye his chest. He wasn't as built as some of his cousins, but he was lean, and he liked how she ogled his muscles.

"I missed this last time you had your shirt off."

"We had more pressing matters. And you were amazing."

She looked at him through her lashes. "You thought so?"

"I have since I met you."

She melted into him, her hands splayed on his back. Nuzzling her neck, he lifted the hem of her dress. The higher he lifted it, the more satiny skin of her legs was visible. He raised it until the lace trim of her underwear slammed lust into him so hard he almost dropped her dress.

Drawing it over her head, he stood still. The garment dropped from his fingers.

Whoa. Tiny scraps of fabric blocked him from paradise. A triangle of underwear covered the apex between her legs, and the sheer material of her bra offered no protection against the delicious view underneath.

His mouth watered to taste her.

Lifting his gaze, he met hers. Her lips parted, her breathing shallow. He enclosed her hand in his and raised it to his mouth. Laying a kiss on each knuckle, he took his time.

"Are you ready for this?"

She tightened her hold on him. "With you, yes."

That was what he needed to hear. He swooped her up. She clung to him as he stretched across the bed with her.

The tiny hook of her bra was nothing. He parted the ends to reveal luminescent skin that begged for his touch. Dusky brown nipples peaked, and he picked one to cover with his mouth, his hand ensconcing the other.

She arched into him, her legs parting to cradle him on either side. He settled in to pleasure her. His fiancée.

She shivered against him as he rolled the tight bud against his tongue. Her hands threaded through his hair. He'd walk proudly around town with messy hair if she was the cause of it.

Switching breasts, he traced his tongue around her nipple before blowing across it.

Her sharp inhale and the tightening of her legs against him made him smile.

She rocked against him. If she was anything like him, she'd been desperately wanting release since their walk in the woods. Both times, they'd done nothing but kiss—a lot—and grope each other through their clothes, but the ache hadn't left him.

He'd take care of her. As he nuzzled his way down, he hooked his fingers under her underwear and rolled them down.

By the time he reached his goal, she'd parted her legs wider to make room for his shoulders. Her sex glistened for him.

He dropped a kiss on her inner thigh. Her leg twitched.

He lifted his gaze off her sweet folds. "I want to taste you."

It sounded like a question. And it kind of was. He didn't want to do anything to ruin the night.

She nodded, catching her pink lower lip between her teeth.

Taking his time, as much as it pained him, he licked and nibbled his way to her sex. Her hands froze in his hair.

"My flower," he murmured and laved his way to her clit.

She gasped and arched when he hit it. This wouldn't take long.

He leisurely stroked her with his tongue. Her hips jerked, and her hands left his hair to twist in the comforter. His zipper cut into his erection, but he relished the bite. Her pleasure would be his undoing otherwise.

She relaxed her knees farther, her body growing fluid, her moans punctuating each swipe of his tongue. When she started thrusting her hips like she needed more, he placed a finger at her entrance.

Could he last through this? Heat flowed off of her. He inserted the tip of his digit into her. Tight walls gripped him. Her juices flooded his tongue, a taste that was uniquely Daisy. His flower.

He withdrew his finger and then slid it in farther. Her panting came faster; her hips bucked.

"I'll take care of you." He clamped his mouth over her clit and thrust into her sex.

"Aaron!" Her orgasm hit. He didn't have to move. She writhed and bucked against his face, riding his finger as her walls convulsed around him. The erotic sight she made was enough to make him come, but he forced down every lustful thought, damn near blanking his mind to hold back his own orgasm.

He wanted to come inside of his fiancée.

When she went limp on the bed with a heavy breath, he pulled away. Grabbing a condom from the drawer, he reared up to his knees.

As he worked the fly of his pants open and shoved them down, he let his gaze wander over her. She was spread wantonly beneath him. Her legs open, her sex wet from him, her nipples pointing to the ceiling. The soft curves of her muscles ready to embrace him.

She pushed hair off her face, her gaze glued to his cock. It twitched under her stare. He paused again, giving her time to signal him it was okay to continue.

She met his gaze, stark desire simmering in her eyes. "I liked that."

The corner of his mouth hitched up. "I did to."

She rose to her elbows and cocked her head. "You called me your flower."

"You're my Daisy."

Her tongue darted out to lick her lips. His cock twitched

again. "Then…I want just you to call me that when I get to the States."

He nodded once. "Done." Anything for her.

She sat up and wrapped her hand around his length. He opened the condom and handed it to her.

This was really going to happen. Would he be a disappointment?

He'd never had sex with someone knowing they'd get married. The magnitude of the moment settled around his shoulders like a winter coat. Would their first time set the whole tone of their relationship? What if he came as soon as he entered her?

As soon as she rolled the condom on, need wiped out his worries. She closed her hand around him and pumped her fist.

His head lolled back, and his eyes closed. "Daisy. I'm struggling as it is. This first round might not last long."

"But there'll be others."

His eyes flew open. Did that sultry tone belong to his flower?

She laid back, leading him to her entrance.

Leaning on an elbow, he held himself above her. She released him, and he hovered at her sex.

Steadily, he pushed inside. She rocked along his length as he backed up and slowly thrust in again. Her tight walls didn't resist, but he worried his girth and her size wouldn't work together. With patience and gritted teeth, he seated himself fully inside.

Another groan left him, and his eyes drifted shut again.

Glorious. There was nothing more a man could ask for. Heat surrounded him. He strained not to piston like a madman.

She embraced him, and he started his rhythm. Slow at first. She needed time to recover from her first orgasm.

Jaw clenched, he pumped his hips. It wasn't long before her legs wrapped around him, greedy for more.

Yes. She was going to come again, and he just might last long enough for it.

"My Daisy," he murmured against her ear. Tremors wracked her body.

He didn't nibble, just pressed his lips against the base of her neck and picked up the pace.

Their rhythm matched perfectly. He shifted the angle to work his hand between them. Like he had with his mouth, he only rested his finger against her clit. Their movement was enough to push her over the edge.

Thank god, because he didn't think he could hold back any longer.

His name ripped from her lips again. He pumped once, twice more, and reared up, throwing his head back, growling her name.

His climax hit so hard he went rigid. She shuddered underneath him as he released.

Finally, his orgasm freed him from its hold and he collapsed over Daisy, but ensured he didn't crush her.

She peppered kisses along his chest as she kneaded her hands over his shoulders and back into his hair.

They stayed like that until their breathing evened out.

He rose to his elbows. Her sex appeal had only grown as she smiled up at him.

She traced his jaw. "Now I'm hungry."

Just like that, he was hard again. "One more time and then we'll order room service."

And after that, he planned to hold her next to him every last minute of their time together.

Aaron woke with a start. Shit—did he miss his flight?

Frowning, he looked around the room. It was still nighttime. The lights were off, but with the blinds open and only the sheers covering the window, ambient light from the city showed Daisy reclined in the uncomfortable hotel chair facing out the window.

"What's wrong?" He rolled up and crossed to stand behind the chair to see what she was seeing. She was still nude, and he'd shed the rest of his clothes within seconds after their first time.

Taillights and headlights streamed through the streets. The buildings around them, other hotels, had scattered lights on throughout each floor. Shadows cast over her face couldn't hide her serious expression.

"I'm thinking about…leaving. You leaving. Then I'll be leaving." She peered up at him. "It's hard not knowing when."

"We'll apply as soon as I get back. Let's plan for three months so at least we have a goal. If it's sooner, great. If it's delayed, we'll get through it. Together."

She reached behind her to clasp his hand. "How did we find each other?"

"I don't care how as long as we did." And that was the truth.

She released a quiet sigh. "No matter what, I will miss Manila. And will miss Manila with you."

Her touch had reignited the blood flow.

He released her hand. "I'll be right back." Padding to the end table, he snatched another condom.

He rolled it on as he walked back. She peeked over the back of the chair to see what he was doing. "Again?"

Was that anticipation in her tone?

"Yes, only this time, we're going to create one last memory of Manila together." He held out his hand. She glanced from it to his straining erection, then accepted the offer.

Once she was standing, he took her place on the chair. Towing her to him, he spun her to face the windows.

"Ah," she said as he tugged her onto his lap, her back to his chest.

His cock was pressed between them as he gathered her thick hair and bared her neck. She eased into him as he kneaded her breasts and nipped the sensitive area at the base of neck.

Brushing one hand down her flat belly, he continued until he reached her clit. She writhed over him, her hands clutching the arms of the chair.

Now. He lifted her at the waist and positioned her over his cock. She lowered herself onto him, and he hissed as she took his length into her. Keeping his hand at her sex, he worked her clit, using his other hand to massage a nipple between his fingers. All the while, he scraped along her neck with his teeth, soothing with his tongue.

Heat flooded his hand. She jerked into him as she orgasmed. He let her ride it out, milking every drop of pleasure. When she was done, he stood, holding her to him as he was still seated inside.

"This will be our memory of Manila." He placed her hands on the glass and gripped her hips.

"Yes," she rasped.

He pumped. He wanted her watching the city, seeing the image of them in the window, of him taking her. His fiancée.

He wanted to fuck her so hard it'd get them through every lonely night until she was back in his arms.

"Daisy." He thrust harder. "Do you see us in the glass?"

"Yes," she whimpered, curving her back to open wider for him.

"This is the memory of us I want to leave you with. You and me in Manila. In this room."

She cried out, bracing herself against the cool surface of the window.

Her sex convulsed around his cock. Hell, she was climaxing already.

That sent him reeling over the peak. His fingers dug into her flesh as he released, bucking, grunting, gritting his teeth. When it was over, he was amazed he could stay standing. From the way Daisy hung against the glass, he was the only thing keeping her upright.

He withdrew and swept her up into his arms. Settling her into bed, he crawled in behind her.

"You and me, flower."

"You and me," she murmured before falling asleep in his embrace.

# CHAPTER 11

*A*aron leaned over the table and poked Lucas's tablet.

"Dammit, Walker. Let me finish," Lucas growled.

The night was quiet at Barley 'n' Hops, making it an ideal place to brainstorm a wedding…for whenever the bride arrived. It'd been six weeks since he'd flown home. It was after the new year, and he and Daisy were in constant contact. She still worked at the internet café. He'd either stay up late to talk with her, or rush home to be by a computer. There were other ways to talk besides Skype, but it was their routine and Daisy insisted on using her discount and not wasting money on anything else.

Each chat was its own torture. Because now he knew her —what she felt like, the sounds she made when he was inside of her. They'd disconnect, and he'd be left with a sense of emptiness, like he wanted to crawl out of his skin and dunk himself in the snow to numb his nerves.

She'd been through her visa interview; they were just waiting for the word. When she was notified, she'd call or email and he'd make her flight arrangements. He'd been meticulous, following each instruction in the application process to a T. Daisy had done the same on her end.

Just the wait was left.

To cheer him up and bribe him into going to the bar with him, Lucas offered to help start planning the wedding. Aaron didn't want to do much without Daisy, but it felt like progress. And Lucas had risen above his own misery to help.

Lucas pulled up the website of the dance hall to search for openings. "Ninety days from when she lands the clock starts ticking right?"

"Yep." And they wouldn't rush. He wanted her to use as much time as was allowed to acclimate.

He rubbed his hands along his thighs. What if she hated Moore? What if she hated his living situation? He hadn't been honest on how his family lived with him. There always seemed to be a better time to tell her.

With the way Mom was acting and the three feet of snow outside and below zero temperatures, he didn't want to bring up the topic of them moving out after Jackson graduated. If Daisy was okay with it, he wouldn't push the issue until after Nicolas graduated next year. A year and a half of one big semi-happy family.

As long as Daisy didn't mind.

Lucas squinted at the online calendar. "Looks like you have the pick of weekends until April hits. Every weekend in April is already booked."

Their drinks were delivered. Aaron glanced up to thank their server. Trina smiled back at him, a little less hostile than the last time he'd run across her in the bar.

"What's this I hear about weddings? Who's getting married?" She slanted a look at the tablet.

Lucas didn't tap out of it but rolled his gaze to Aaron.

Hell, he and his entire crew of relatives hadn't spoken outside of the family about Daisy. When someone had asked about his trip, he couldn't hold back his smile, but he'd kept his private life private. He wanted his fiancée by his side before he told anyone.

Aaron scrolled through his brain for an excuse. The four cousins he farmed with were married, but there was Travis's brother Justin, who'd recently moved back to town. "We were teasing Justin about settling down now that he's come back to farm with us."

She nodded and shrugged. "That's right. I didn't believe it until I saw him driving a fancy-ass truck around."

Yeah, Justin had returned with a healthy bank account.

Lucas took a swig from his beer bottle. That was a good sign. He wasn't hitting the hard stuff—yet. "When do you get off work, Trina?"

Her eyes narrowed. "When do you go home to your wife?"

A muscle clenched in Lucas's jaw, but he covered it with a cavalier tone. "Uh, never. The divorce papers arrived last week."

Trina's eyes flew wide. "I'm so sorry." She blinked again. Aaron knew how she felt. Lucas hadn't said a thing.

"Surprised? I didn't quit farming, and she didn't leave Dr. Do-me, so I filed. She still thinks I'll move to town and woo her back. Not gonna happen." He took another drink and swayed toward her. "Does that change anything?"

Not all of the sympathy drained out of her face, but she did smile. "No. Sorry, again. That baggage hasn't been unpacked." She switched her gaze to Aaron, a hint of suggestion in her eyes.

He looked away. A nice corner he painted himself into.

Lucas swiveled his gaze between the two of them until he settled on Aaron and cocked a brow.

Aaron's choices were to sidestep the conversation and let Trina think he passed because Lucas had hit on her first, or to be honest without throwing his privacy away and hope she didn't inquire further. "I'm seeing someone, Trina."

She recoiled. Did she have to look so surprised. "So that's why you haven't been in here in a while."

He nodded, not trusting himself to not spill every detail about Daisy, from her laugh to how much she loved her mom's cooking. A sense of betrayal plagued him, but it was for Daisy's benefit. Her new start couldn't be shadowed by opinions and speculations.

"That's awesome," Trina said. "Holler when you two want a refill." She wandered away without looking at either of them.

Lucas glared at his beer.

Interpreting Lucas's behavior was becoming another task on his never-ending list. "If you have a thing for her, why did you keep pushing her and I together?"

"Cuz I was married, jackass." Lucas tapped his tablet screen back on. "And I didn't think she'd be so hung up on you."

"She's not. I'm not the reason she's been avoiding you for months."

"I know," Lucas growled. "I should've told people I was divorcing sooner, but I'm like you with Daisy. I don't want people in my business."

"Maybe you should quit women for a while. You know, to give yourself time to deal."

"I'd love to deal all by myself while coming here to drink alone because you're stupid over your fiancée." Bitterness dripped from his words. Lucas was the only non-relative Aaron had told and when the dam broke, well, he'd gushed about Daisy.

The tablet screen blinked off again. This wasn't the time to talk about wedding plans. He hunched over his drink.

Someday he could shout out his good news. "Tell me about the divorce."

~

Dalisay disconnected the call with Ina. Two months had passed since Aaron had left and five weeks had passed since Ina had moved into her work place as a live-in housekeeper.

She looked around the empty room. She'd downgraded to a room with only one bed after Ina moved out. Aaron covered the cost and she'd chosen a hotel that was safe and clean, but plain and not expensive. The commute to work was farther, but there was nothing else she had to do with her time other than sleep.

Checking her email, she frowned as she stared at the lack of notification that her visa packet was waiting for her. It could take up to three months. One more month to go crazy.

Killing time on the computer only helped it pass a microsecond faster. She'd scrolled through every webpage about Moore, her soon-to-be new home. Aaron had said it was smaller than Solano, but Moore didn't even top out at ten thousand people. And he'd said it was close enough to larger cities, but they were kilometers away.

*Miles.* She had to get used to miles and pounds now.

She'd get her license and drive, but commuting that far to another town each day boggled her mind. But he'd said the time to get from Moore to a larger town probably wasn't much different than when her trip to work was delayed due to extra-congested traffic. *Only a fraction of that number of vehicles are on our roads. The only time we're bumper to bumper is during a parade.*

Unless, he'd said, the weather was bad.

Snow! A new experience, if she got to Moore before the thaw. *It can snow as late as April, sometimes even in May.*

So many new adventures waiting for her, and she was stuck in a hotel room. She'd finally put up the Do Not Disturb sign so she'd have something to clean to get a break from watching TV.

She had the night off, and she wanted to scream in frustration. When was the last time she'd been alone like this? In university, she'd had classmates and roommates. She'd met her ex. After leaving, her friends had moved on, her fiancé had found someone else, but Ina had moved in. Still, she'd been alone before. Why was this different?

Because she and Aaron had made memories and she couldn't escape them. Didn't want to escape them, but she could no longer go anywhere without thinking about him.

Go to a restaurant: *What's new that Aaron could try here?*

A gift shop: *Does Aaron need any more souvenirs for his brothers?*

Look out the hotel window—well, that made more than her heart ache. The last night they'd spent together had done more than create a memory. It had cemented their relationship. It was real. They were real. A couple engaged to be married. And they were living apart.

Ugh. If she was going to be pathetic tonight, she might as well crawl between the covers and turn the TV on.

Settled in for the evening, she skimmed through channels and watched a few shows. Her eyelids grew heavy. On compulsion, she reached for her phone and checked for messages and updates.

She bolted up with a gasp. A wide smile broke out.

Finally!

# CHAPTER 12

The plane bumped down onto the runway. Dalisay released her hold on the armrests and peered out the window. Outside was pitch black, interspersed with brilliant beams of lights from the runway and miniscule airport. She scanned around, looking across the aisle and over the only other seat in the entire row of this—what had Aaron called it? Puddle-jumper?

A few large hangars were visible, and she'd caught sight of an office-type building as the plane swung around. The airport?

So not like Manila.

The same thought had echoed through her head when she'd landed in Seattle. The bustle of the people was familiar, and while she'd only ever been in Manila's airport, it had still been an airport. The same with Minneapolis.

But the large aircrafts that had carried her overseas on her first flight ever, then to her next stop in Minnesota, hadn't inspired the anxiety as the small craft had. Every bump and jerk of the plane was magnified as she'd flown from Minneapolis to Moore.

*The plane will be nothing but a puddle-jumper, but it'll fly you right into my town and you won't have to face hours of driving. We never know how well the weather will behave this time of year.*

She might've chanced it.

Fatigue seeped into every bone and muscle. The jangle of nerves brewing a storm in her belly had no resistance.

The plane rolled to a stop. She was here. She shivered, an action that had nothing to do with the shadows of large piles of snow outside the window. The swirl of anticipation in her stomach needed an outlet.

She drew in a ragged breath. The passengers around her passed her polite smiles, but the question in their eyes spoke a lot. *Who are you? What are you doing in Moore?*

Aaron had said that Moore was large enough to not know everybody, but small enough to know a lot of people. When she'd asked him how many people from the Philippines lived there, he'd gone quiet.

*None that I know of. But I'm sure they do.*

So what he was trying not to say was that she'd stand out. Eventually, they'd talked about it. The kind of reaction she might get around town. The questions that might be asked. How she thought she'd feel. He was worried.

To go from a city where she was less than a blip in the day to one where everyone would know her hadn't been intimidating twenty-four hours ago. But if it was like this flight, where she received curious glances, then it shouldn't be so bad.

The door opened and they all stood. She slung her backpack over her shoulder. The short line couldn't move fast enough. A blast of cold air flowed down the aisle. She shivered and this time, it was definitely from the frigid air.

She'd worn the heaviest jacket she had, but it offered no more protection than her canvas shoes would from the snow.

This was so not Manila.

A gasp ripped from her as she stepped into the night. Her teeth clattered. Oh god. It was like the wind was eating her face off.

She tucked her head into her collar and scurried behind the other passengers into the building. Barely noticing the quaint room they piled through to gape at the tidy interior, she ran into a wall of chest.

Hard arms came around her and the previous two months of anxiety and excitement coalesced in her throat. She shoved hard, for the little good it did.

"Daisy, it's me."

That voice. Deep, easy, and familiar. Instantly, her body calmed and melted into Aaron. She slumped against him, not just out of relief. He was warm.

"Are you shivering?" He released her to shrug off the heavy tan coat he wore. Worn and faded in spots, she doubted its ability, but once he took her backpack and slung the coat around her shoulders she was encapsulated in a weighty comfort that smelled like Aaron and fresh air.

"Oh, that is much better." She smiled and absorbed her fiancé standing in front of her with her bag now on his back. "Hi, Aaron."

His lopsided grin flipped her heart. "Hey." He bent and kissed her. Their lips clung together for a heartbeat before he pulled away. "Let's get your bag and go home."

He slung his arm around her. His knit long-sleeved shirt didn't look like it'd stand up to the weather, but she couldn't give up his jacket yet. Maybe he'd brought an extra?

The airport didn't have a luggage belt. A door opened and the attendant wheeled in bags.

She hung back, still pasted to Aaron's side while everyone got theirs. An older man from the flight nodded a greeting at Aaron, then looked at her. Stared was more like it.

She was too tired to try to smile or guess what an appropriate response would be. Her ring was on her finger, and that should answer enough questions.

Aaron grabbed her suitcase. "Just one?"

"Ina moved everything to her new place."

He led her outside.

She tugged on his arm. "Wait. Do you want your coat back?"

"Absolutely not. The truck's been running this whole time anyway. I wanted to keep it warm for you."

She didn't argue as they stepped back into the wind. It robbed her of breath. She screwed up her face against it and followed Aaron. The air even smelled cold, like a giant cube of ice around her, tinged with exhaust.

Looking around the parking lot, almost every car was running. Billowy clouds of exhaust filtered into the night. That was from the cold and not engine trouble?

They approached a truck that could rival any Jeepney for size. The cab had four doors and she'd need a ladder to get inside.

Aaron opened the door. "Here. Use the running boards and the 'oh shit' handle to climb in."

"The what?" He gave her a boost and pointed to the frame.

"The 'oh shit' handle. You know, for when you have to hold on and say…"

She chuckled. "I get it."

Aaron closed the door. The warmth of the cab seeped in and his coat swamped her. She tore her gaze off him to look around the cab.

Papers were piled between her and the driver's seat. Magazines that looked like ads stacked amid envelopes and work gloves. His phone had slipped off the console and lay upside down in a drink holder.

Aaron got in on the other side. "Sorry about the mess. Would you believe I cleaned it up?"

"It's not that bad."

He smirked. "Then don't look in the back seat."

"You're messy. It's okay." She didn't care. They were together again.

"No, it's not. I'm just busy." He reached over to stretch the seatbelt around her, then clicked himself in.

The clock display said it was nine thirty. She was too tired to figure out what time it was at home.

Wait. She was home.

Resting her head on the seat, she alternated between watching Aaron drive because he was too good to be true and viewing her new home.

So few buildings. But lights stretched in front of them. They must be a few miles out of town.

She sat forward as they drove into Moore. Sprawling gas stations that took up an entire block each bordered both sides of the highway. And the highway! Only a few other vehicles heading in each direction were on the road. This was more like Solano. Except the stories-high street lamps and the multitude of fluorescent signs set it apart.

He drove past restaurants and banks, and all too soon they were heading back down a dark highway.

"On a scale of one to ten, how tired are you?" he asked. They hadn't spoken all through Moore as if he'd known she'd only want to gawk.

"Eleven. I understand why you slept in the day you arrived in Manila. I think I could sleep for a week." Part of it might have to do with the stress of moving and finding herself unemployed. No evening shift to stress over left her drained.

"You can sleep that long if you'd like. I'll be around.

February's the month I try to catch up on any repair jobs that Brock couldn't get to."

The cousin who was their mechanic. She was going to meet these people she'd heard all about. Had Aaron been as intimidated when he'd met Peejong? He hadn't shown it.

"I…um, we never talked about where you'd sleep when you got here."

She quirked a brow at him. No, they hadn't. It seemed odd now that they were each heading to his house to go to bed.

"There's a spare room upstairs. You can have my room with the nice bed and I'll sleep in the spare, until you know, we're married."

Was she interpreting this correctly? "We're not sleeping together until we're married?"

Disappointment trailed through her. The arrangement made perfect sense.

"I want to do whatever is comfortable for you. No pressure." He shifted in his seat and stared into the darkness.

The snow mounded along the edge of the highway. The only thing she could see besides that were metal fence posts and thin wire strung between them. And some rows of trees here and there.

"I also haven't been completely honest."

She stilled. A shot of adrenaline flooded her veins. "About what?"

"How close my parents and brothers live. They're in the basement."

"Oh." Four other people lived under the roof. Wasn't that what she'd wanted to avoid with her uncle?

He turned off the highway onto a dirt road and pulled to a stop. "I understand if you hold it against me. But my parents moving back in with me has prevented any other relationship from getting serious. Then when I met you, I wanted you to get to know me before I told you." His eyes were earnest in the glow of the dashboard lights. "Only when I got to know you, I was afraid it'd scare you off."

His words rang with truth and apology. Tension radiated through his face. His jaw was tight, his shoulders rigid.

"Okay." Her foggy mind couldn't think of anything else to say. Was it okay? She didn't know enough yet. Would it have scared her off if he'd told her? Probably not. Aaron inspired her to consider a lot of things she never thought she'd do. Like moving across the world to a place with over a hundred-degree temperature difference.

"Okay?" he asked. "Like okay, or you're too tired to care and might care tomorrow?"

"Just okay. I don't know your family to know if it's a problem. I guess you met me when I lived with my mom."

"But I didn't move in with you."

She giggled at the picture of him planted at the tiny square table she and Ina ate around. He'd make it look like it came from a playset.

"Take me home, Aaron."

AARON PACED THE KITCHEN. The floor creaked where the hardwood butted the carpet seam. He spun and stopped. Mom eyed him from the other entrance into the room. She'd dressed in something other than sweat pants today.

"Do we get to meet her yet?" she asked, looking over his shoulder.

"She's still sleeping." He'd strongly suggested his family park it downstairs until he got her in and settled. She'd passed out snuggled into his bed within seconds, and he'd watched her almost long enough to be classified as creepy, even if they were engaged.

But long black hair spread across his pillow hit him in the solar plexus. Her slight body wrapped in his freshly washed sheets. The woman he was going to marry.

He'd camped in the spare room on the rock-hard bed that would offer better comfort if it were used as kindling for a bonfire.

"It's ten already. If she wants to switch her hours, she should get up now." Mom poured herself some juice.

It was ten in the morning and Mom had just come upstairs. Yet he'd been up when his brothers had headed to school. "She'll have plenty of time to adjust."

"And you're going to make the floor creak with your pacing for another three hours waiting for her to wake?"

He ducked his head. "If I have to."

Mom cocked her head and scrutinized him the same way she used to before family pictures. "I'm sure you're not surprised that I doubted this whole thing, but I see how much you're invested. I hope she's as sweet as you say."

"I couldn't do her justice."

Mom drained her juice and left her cup by the sink. The dishwasher was right underneath, but he'd take care of it later.

She was turning toward the entrance to the stairs. "Well, I'm heading back down— Oh."

Aaron twisted around. Emerging from the hallway was a timid Daisy. She was brushing her hand down the length of her hair as if self-conscious that she had bedhead, which looked adorable. The long-sleeved shirt she wore said "Seattle" and her black leggings were from the previous night.

She smiled, but her eyes screamed deer in the tractor's spotlight. "Hello, Mrs. Walker."

Mom didn't cross to Daisy. She wasn't a hugger. She wasn't much of anything lately, but that was another problem. "Call me Lori, please. It's nice to finally meet you. How was your trip?"

"It was great." Daisy's voice was hardly audible. "Very pleasant."

He jumped in before things got any more awkward. "Hungry? I can't cook eggs like your mom, but I'll try."

Daisy smiled at him. "I can cook them if you show me around. But first, where's...?" Pink tinted her cheeks.

Mom saved him. "The bathroom is the second door to the right behind you."

"Thank you." Daisy disappeared back down the hall.

"So, that's her." Mom's expression was guarded.

"Yep. Hey, do you have a winter coat she can borrow? I think we'll have to go pick up some cold weather clothing for her."

"Sure. I'll set a few things at the top of the stairs."

Aaron bit down on his tongue. There was no *don't worry about it, I'll take her shopping. It'll be a great way to get to know my future daughter-in-law.* Nor *let me make a list of what she'll need.* He didn't even get a full trip up the stairs.

He'd take it personally, but that was the way Mom had been for years now.

"Where's Dad?" he called as his mom went down the stairs.

"In the shop."

Thankfully, someone was working if he was taking the week off. He worked on Daisy's breakfast until she appeared without a sound, wearing a fresh pair of tight jeans that he'd never seen her in and her Seattle sweater. A good choice for this climate.

"Can I help?" she asked.

He gave her a smile. "Nah. It's my turn to wow you with my cooking skills."

She circled the kitchen and peeked into the living room. "This is what it looks like in the daylight."

"Pretty simple." And old. Trying to see it through her eyes, the outdated 90's decor was glaring, along with the faded carpet and drapes. He'd planned to upgrade a little each year, but he'd gotten so busy, it'd fallen to the end of the priority list.

"It's nice," she said. "And there's a lower level?"

He slid their breakfast, brunch for him, onto a couple of plates. Setting the pan back down, he frowned. Whenever he'd eaten with Daisy and Mari, they'd had an abundance of fresh produce. Well, his eggs were homegrown, but that was all on the plate.

He could get fruit and veggies at the grocery store, but the prices were obscene this time of year and the quality dipped. He had a fridge full of oranges and apples, though.

While he prepped those, he rambled. "My brothers are at school and everyone is working right now, but I thought we could go to town and get a coat and some sweaters for you. Boots, too. Gloves and hat. Do you have any of that?"

"Not really, no." She looked so petite standing in the middle of his kitchen with no idea what to do.

He gestured to the table. "Go ahead and have a seat. I'll bring our plates."

Instead of sitting, she came to him and helped carry the food over. "This looks good."

He wanted to use her answer. *Not really, no.* Scrambled eggs and orange slices weren't the food he wanted to impress his fiancée with.

"We can run to the grocery store, too. To get any stuff you like."

She paused with her fork over her plate. "Do you think your family would like my cooking?"

He chuckled. "My brothers and I split the cooking around

here. Sometimes Dad makes his chili. But our first rule is there's no complaining."

The awkwardness lingered as they ate. She didn't comment on his food. Was she following the rule, or did she really think it tasted like more than blah warm goo?

He snagged her plate when she was done. "Mind meeting my dad before we run to town?"

"It's no problem." She met him at the sink and prepared to wash.

"Oh, we have a dishwasher. Just leave them. One of us will load them later."

Her tiny apartment hadn't had one, and it'd only been her and Mari. His family probably used as many dishes in one day as those two had all week.

Before they got going, he had to make sure they were on the same page. "When we get to town, you might get introduced to others. If it ever gets overwhelming, just give me a nudge or something."

She considered him. "Were you overwhelmed at Solano?"

He lifted a shoulder. "There was too much new stuff to take in, so, no. I enjoyed meeting your family. But it was also like a vacation for me. This is your new..."

She met his gaze. "My new life."

"Weird, huh?"

"Surreal." Her gaze drifted away before she looked back. "I missed you."

He pulled her toward him until he could hook his hands behind her waist. "So much." He dropped his head for a real kiss, not the quick peck he limited himself to the night before. As long as she reciprocated.

And she did. Her hands hugged his shoulders. His hands crept lower. He just wanted to touch her again. It'd been so long.

"Here's the jacket and some other things I could find," his mother called from the stairwell.

Daisy jerked back, her flush deepening. But Mom didn't come all the way up. It would've been too much work.

"She'll probably swim in them." Mom's voice faded. Daytime TV called to her.

Daisy sighed and buried her head in his shirt.

Note to self: she wasn't comfortable with PDAs in front of his family yet.

He grinned and rubbed Daisy's back. "You might want to throw another shirt under that sweater before I show you around. Then we'll go to town."

He led her toward the stairs. "The basement entrance and mudroom are over here. The backdoor is just around the corner." Stooping to grab the clothing, he looked over the selection. None of it was Daisy's simple style.

Hell, his mom even threw in an ugly Christmas sweater. At least there was a winter coat, the kind with the outer shell and fleece insert. Perfect.

When he turned, she was staring at the pictures on the wall that led past the kitchen to the hallway. Shoving the pile under one arm, he pointed out people.

"This one is from the day me and the guys signed for the business." He touched on each guy as he said their names.

"It's nicer than the tiny pictures on your phone." She moved to the next photo.

He tapped on the glass. "This was the last official family photo we took, like ten years ago. Did I show you Jackson's senior picture?"

"He looks a lot more like you."

"Yeah, but he's stockier and way more shy than I ever was." He handed her the coat and dug out a hat and gloves from his mom's stash. "Put these on. There's a pair of boots by the door."

"Are you sure she doesn't mind?" She held the coat up and inspected all the zippers and pockets.

"She's lived here her whole life. I bet she has at least five winter coats, eight light jackets, and probably a hundred sweaters."

She eyed the dark pink and white jacket for another second before swinging it over her shoulders. "I can't believe how cold it was last night."

"It'll be like that for a few more days, then warm up to single digits." He showed her around the rest of the upstairs since it'd been too late for a tour when they'd gotten in. There wasn't much to see, but he wanted her to feel…at home.

Before they went outside, he geared her up with the rest of her cold weather items. By the time he was done, she was the best snow bunny he could've ever dreamed of. She'd rolled the bottom of her wool knit hat and had matching gloves that her hands must swim in. Mom's calf boots gave her enough protection to keep her feet and legs warm.

They wandered outside. She gasped as the air hit her face.

He glanced back and caught the end of her grimace. She was about to say something, but stopped and blew a lungful of air that puffed into a cloud. Then giggled.

He'd grown up in this weather and not once had he played with his breath. Maybe as a kid and he didn't remember.

Imagining what is was like to experience it for the first time seemed impossible, but she was expressive enough that he understood.

"It's so cold." She tucked her face into the collar of her jacket. "I suppose you're used to it."

"I don't think we're ever used to it. These kinds of temps shock the system no matter what. We just adapt to dealing with it."

A dusting of snow had fallen overnight. Their boots crunched on the surface like they were walking across a Styrofoam egg carton to the shop where his truck was parked. She waited by the door while he hopped in to start it and slid back out.

"It'll warm up while I show you around." He hated keeping her outside so long, but this was her new home.

He walked her through the shop, into the front of the barn, and past the large silver metal cylinder grain bins.

"Those are massive," she breathed. The tip of her nose was red. Cute as hell. "Are they full of grain?"

"Depends on the time of year."

She nodded and spun in a slow circle to get a panoramic view of the property. "All this is yours?"

"Everything the house and out-buildings are sitting on, yes. And twenty more acres. All the fields and pastures are Walker Five land, so I'm a co-owner of those. You'll get a better view of all that when we head to town. Ready?"

His ego screamed its impatience. Months of keeping his fiancée a secret. And he could finally introduce her to people. They might wonder how he and Daisy met, but there was nothing wrong with meeting online. No one had to know it was a dating site meant to find a spouse. He sure wasn't going to tell anyone.

# CHAPTER 13

*D*aisy tossed the last bag into the back seat of the pickup. She'd seen the space a few other times, but each time it hit her that, wow, it was really messy.

And why would that bother her? She'd always been a tidy kid and hadn't changed as an adult. Would it bother her if her husband was a slob?

Yes, but she didn't get that impression from Aaron. But all he'd had in his hotel room was his suitcase and she'd only seen it the last night before he'd left when it had been packed.

So messy! Articles of clothing were strewn across the seats and on the floor. Vehicles parts, or maybe equipment for the goliath machinery in his shop, was half buried. Baseball caps that had Walker Five logos on them peeked out. At least three.

A pair of overalls and an additional winter coat topped the pile like a fluffy, oil stained cherry.

She hadn't known that side of Aaron, hadn't gotten exposed to this side of him. He was still Aaron, but now he was...more? Different? It didn't help they'd been apart for over two months.

Shutting the door, she mentally shook herself. They'd grown close quickly online. Their chemistry had been more than a slow burn to an explosive goodbye. They'd get back there.

Aaron had her door open, waiting. She slid into the toasty seat. In town, the weather was the same, but the effect was dampened from all the buildings and short distances to walk from a parking spot.

She shook her head. The longest they'd had to scurry between his pickup and an entrance was less than a hundred meters. Definitely not like Manila, but more like her hometown of Solano. But for as long as they'd been in town, through three stores and soon the grocery store, she hadn't seen one bus.

"Where's the public transportation?" she asked when Aaron climbed in. He'd said she'd learn to drive after moving here, but how would her feet reach the pedals in this beast?

His easy shrug soothed her brimming anxiety. She was used to stepping out the door and having a variety of methods available to her. Some better than others, some more accessible. But they were there.

"They're around," he said.

She kept watch. Cars and pickups. Delivery trucks. Depending where they were in town, semis would cross their path, or cattle trucks like the one parked in one of Aaron's massive shops.

It was her first day in a new country. She needed to soak in her surroundings and enjoy Aaron's presence.

Within minutes, they were at a grocery store. A warehouse-style supermarket, similar but larger than she was used to in Solano. In Manila, she'd popped in and out of smaller markets, grabbing only what she'd need for a day or two. Then Ina had moved in and taken over much of the shopping.

She took her time perusing the aisles. Aaron wandered next to her, answering any questions she had.

"Oh, Ina loves these." She grabbed a package of coconut macaroons and added them to her cart. "We don't have this brand at home."

Aaron indicated the cart. "You can get something for yourself, you know."

So far, she'd grabbed random food items for Ina to sample. Food was her thing. It was hard not to think of her in a grocery store.

"You miss her."

The sadness must've shown on her face. "Yes. I missed her before I left, like I did when I first went to university. Now that I'm here…" She returned to strolling down the aisle. If she didn't move, tears might spring up. She didn't need to be crying on her first day in America. "It's different."

"We can send her as big a box as you want."

His caring words ignited a warm glow that threatened to overheat her in the coat. She removed her hat and set it in the shopping cart with her gloves. She steeled herself for the lingering glances from strangers. It wasn't as bad when she was covered from nearly head to toe.

She sensed no hostility, but it wasn't in her nature to stand out—ever. Going out with Aaron in Manila and Solano had been similar, but he'd been the one others had stared at too long.

She grabbed a few meal staples that Aaron might not have stocked. They reached the produce section. She catalogued a meal in her head to prepare for Aaron and his family. Picking through, she chose the ingredients. The store had most of what she was looking for. When she thumbed through jalapeños, Aaron leaned over her shoulder.

"Only get what you'll eat. I can guarantee none of the rest will touch that."

But they were only jalapeños. "Nothing?"

"Well, maybe the boys will try it, but I've rarely seen them use the pepper shaker. Eh, go ahead and try it. It'll be good for them."

As she bagged her peppers, a swaggering man about Aaron's age approached. His gaze swept her from head to toe, but not in a leery way. Curiosity, but more personal than others around town. He was dressed similar to Aaron with blue jeans, work boots, and a heavy winter coat that was left hanging open while he was in the store. Attractive, with mussed brown hair and eyes as light a brown as a walnut shell. But he didn't give her the stirrings in her belly like Aaron did.

The man addressed Aaron when he approached. "Where have you been? I've sent you a text I don't know how many times."

Aaron frowned and withdrew his phone. "I sent you a message back. Oh." He squinted at the screen and tapped it. "There. *Now* I sent the message. Lucas, this is Dalisay."

Lucas held out his hand and she shook it. Somehow, she ended up pressed against Aaron's side. Had he pulled her in, or had she sought refuge from the scrutiny? Aaron had talked about his good friend Lucas. She struggled to recall the details.

"How's Moore treating you?" Lucas asked.

"It's been very well, thank you."

Lucas nodded and peered at her like he didn't know what else to say. He switched back to Aaron. "You two need to come out and catch me up on everything. Last week, you didn't mention she was coming."

"I— We didn't know then."

"Well, that's awesome. Why don't we go to Barley 'n' Hops this weekend? Name the night and maybe I'll have a shot with Trina when she sees you're taken."

Aaron stiffened against her. The comment seeped in. Trina was…interested in Aaron? Or had they been a thing?

The brutal question arose. How much did she trust Aaron? They'd talked about relationships, and their expectations in one, and he knew of the reason behind her failed engagement. But she hadn't outright asked him if he'd quit seeing others.

"No—" Aaron started.

"Yes. It sounds like a fun place." She smiled at the two men.

Lucas's brows popped up like he'd been expecting resistance. "Great. Saturday, then. Eight o'clock." He sauntered off with a bunch of bananas tucked under an arm.

"That went…weird," Aaron muttered, scowling at his friend's back. He blinked. "And it sounded really incriminating for me, didn't it?"

She went for nonplussed, but probably failed.

"I'll explain on the ride home." He bent to whisper in her ear, his warm breath caressing her skin. She missed that. "Too many ears listening around here."

He didn't sound like a guy caught in a two-timing lie. Her tension drained, and she finished her shopping.

Back in his truck, he explained about hooking up with Trina and getting the brush-off, and Lucas's odd behavior around the woman, before and after his wife left him.

There was more to Lucas than his blunt behavior, and if he was a friend of Aaron's, then she wanted to get to know him. Saturday night. Aaron said he'd already made it clear he was taken, and Daisy would make sure it was obvious. She wasn't losing another fiancé.

aron twirled his spaghetti around his fork. Nicolas had cooked supper tonight and they all sat around the table. Daisy had met all of his family and his best friend. Tomorrow, he'd subject her to his cousins and their wives. With the size of his family, the slower the better.

"How was shopping today?" Mom asked. Puffy bags rimmed under her eyes and the aura of haggardness around her was more apparent than before. Was she not feeling well?

Daisy nodded around a mouthful of noodles.

"We ran into Lucas." He stabbed into a meatball. The encounter had left Aaron with a "thrown under the bus" feeling. There was nothing to be ashamed of, and there were women in Moore he had slept with—all before Daisy—but pointing Trina out on Daisy's first day here was underhanded. And he had to face that business Saturday night.

Jackson spoke up. "I heard he's getting divorced? And here I thought he was oblivious to how big of a bitch Shaylee is."

"Jackson!" Aaron snapped. Daisy chewed next to him, riveted to the conversation.

His brother shrugged. "Whatever. Maybe she was nice to you. I started asking for a different hygienist. My teeth throbbed for days after she cleaned them. I made a comment once and was afraid she'd shank me with her little pointy tool."

Nicolas snorted. "Totally. I told her that she must polish teeth with the tears of her patients."

Aaron was about to admonish them for trashing Shaylee around Daisy but couldn't stop his chuckle. What Nicolas said was probably too close to true. "I never went to her. Thought it'd be weird."

And he'd gotten tired of always getting asked when he was going to settle down. *Who's the next to marry into the Walker empire, Aaron?* She always said it around Lucas, too. Mind fucked him good, and Aaron hadn't noticed it until now. No wonder Lucas used him to make himself look better. How long before Aaron got his friend back?

The conversation fell quiet.

His dad snuck furtive glances at Daisy but didn't address her. She was going to be his daughter-in-law, and the man who'd raised all boys apparently didn't know what to do.

Jackson broke the silence. "I have a date to prom."

They all stopped and gaped at him. Jackson never had a date. Daisy looked around the table and set her fork down.

Nicolas noticed her uncertainty first. "'I have a date' are not words Jackson's ever spoken before," he said to her.

"Congratulations," Daisy said with a small smile.

Jackson beamed. "Thanks. It's not for like, two months, but girls like to prepare I guess."

Nicolas grinned. "Girls like a lot of things you don't know about."

Aaron threw his napkin at Nicolas. Might as well let Daisy see how they really communicated. "Girls like a lot of things you'd better not know about, or I'm having a long talk with Emily's dad."

"It's her mom you have to worry about." Nicolas lobbed it back. "Who's gonna be on your arm, Jackson?"

"Delaney Smythe."

Nicolas barked a laugh. "You think you can get Del in a dress? Good luck with that."

"I don't care what she wears. It's her prom." Jackson shoved another load of pasta into his mouth.

Mom pushed her plate aside, her mouth tight. "A wedding and the prom, all within the next few months?" She turned to him, her gaze flickering to a quiet Daisy, no life in her eyes. "Have you two started planning?"

What was Mom's problem? Any of his aunts would be ecstatic. His cousins had told him that they were being bugged constantly for updates on him and Daisy. When he'd gone to prom, Mom had beamed and gone to help him pick out a tux. She hadn't broken a smile when Jackson made his news. His brother hadn't gone last year, and Nicolas would probably go with his girlfriend.

Dad was nodding and chewing, as if he liked being part of the conversation and was happy if they were happy.

Aaron stared down at the remains of his meal. Guess he'd plan on tux shopping, or whatever the hell guys wore to prom nowadays. Knowing Jackson, he'd wear jeans if his date said it was fine. A nice sport coat then?

Dammit, his parents should be doing that. He had a wedding to plan. While a simple justice of the peace would have to do, he wanted a celebration with his family and friends. He'd been through all of theirs.

He stretched his arm across the back of Daisy's chair. "We have three months to plan. We don't need to reserve a church, so it's just the reception and dance."

Mom's brows crinkled. "No church wedding? I know you

mentioned it, but you two couldn't come up with a compromise?"

He curled his fingers around Daisy's tight shoulder. She didn't speak up, so he filled in their decision for Mom. "We're on a deadline for the marriage. She doesn't need to change her address, her home, and her religion all at the same time. Once we're married, she can check out our church, check out the Catholic ones in town, and make her decision." He shrugged. "I'll go where she goes."

"Better get used to that line of thinking." Dad snickered and pushed back from the table. It must've been some signal to the others. They all picked up their plates and left.

Clangs of dishes getting set on the counter sounded from the kitchen. Aaron rolled his eyes to the ceiling. He'd emptied the dishwasher earlier.

Aaron rose and lent a hand to Daisy. "Jackson cooked, so he's immune from cleanup. I'll take care of this if you want to watch TV or something."

"I'll help."

"No, you don't—"

She grasped his elbow and rose to her tiptoes. He wasn't passing up a kiss. Their first real one since she'd returned.

Her warm lips landed on his, and he snaked his arms around her. What had he been going to say?

She was back in his arms. Heat flooded his body. God, he could take her on the table. The counter. He didn't care where.

But he couldn't, and wasn't that his curse?

He didn't push it further. Left it at tasting her, holding her, then leaned back. Her eyelids lifted, and they stared at each other. Yeah, doing dishes was going to be a whole lot more fun from now on.

～

THE PROXIMITY to Aaron was killing her. Dalisay had been in town for five days. It was Saturday, date night, and she was in Aaron's room—her room—*their* room—getting ready.

Except for a lingering kiss here and there, they hadn't done more than lay together. How could they with everyone home? She couldn't cry out too loudly during an orgasm and face them the next morning. Waiting until they were wed might be for the best. It'd feel less incriminating.

They had yet to talk about when they'd get married. He wanted to plan a celebration, and she desired that for him. Loss tugged at her heart. Ina would miss both the wedding and the celebration.

They'd talked about that before Ina moved to her new job. Pictures, stories, more pictures was all Ina had asked for. And a promise to fly back after the first grandbaby arrived. Ina had teared up before she'd finished the request. Then Dalisay had started crying and they weren't able to continue the conversation.

She held up a new sweater she hadn't worn yet. Aaron had bought her five. He'd said they had a month, maybe two, of typical winter weather. After that, she might still think it was terribly cold until June compared to what she'd grown up with.

The varying pale blues in the horizontal stripes on the garment didn't scream hot date, but paired with jeggings and the fuzzy top boots she'd gotten, it'd be cute and keep her warm. She chewed on her lower lip. One of her belts might make it more stylish.

Just in case that old not-really girlfriend of Aaron's was there. Nip any potential problems before they had a chance to flourish. There were no tender feelings toward her ex, but his betrayal had left a crater of an impression and it was fueling her drive to see the woman who dared hit on Aaron.

And console herself that nothing had happened while she'd been cooped up in that lonely hotel room.

Shrugging into her clothing, she swiveled to check herself in the mirror. She hated the thought of going outside without a hat, but hat head was real and tonight wasn't the night to sport it. Her hair was combed to hang straight down her back.

She was meeting all of his cousins. Not just the ones he farmed with. No, Aaron had turned the night into her unveiling. The cousins he worked with and their spouses, the other cousins that lived in town, and any friends other than Lucas.

The night had almost been canceled. Snow had fallen all night long. Daisy stared out the window until her breath fogged it over watching the guys push snow back and forth out of his massive driving lane, the courtyard-like area that the house and shops and barn were set around. The tractor he drove was as tall as the house, with a big bucket on the front that scooped and pounded the snow into large piles.

Nicolas, Jackson, and Aaron's dad ran the smaller snow blower and shoveled the walkways that the tractor couldn't reach. Lori hadn't breached the top of the stairs. How did she stand it down there all day?

A tap on the door broke into her thoughts.

Aaron called from the other side. "I pulled the truck to the front of the house so it's ready when you are. No rush."

"I'm ready." She opened the door and her heart thumped to a stop.

He wore a nicer hat than normal, one from his company, and it complemented his eyes. So did the crisp navy shirt he wore. His lanky but muscular frame was more obvious in the fresh pair of jeans.

Purely delectable. Had he looked different in Manila or

was he growing more handsome the longer she was around him?

He whistled, and an appreciative eyebrow cocked. "You look nice." Nice sounded so plain, but not tonight. The way he said it made her feel like she was killing the runway.

"I was just thinking the same."

He grinned, and her stomach flopped. "I clean up okay. It just doesn't happen too often." He snaked an arm out and pulled her close. "But now that you're here, I'll make more of an effort."

Their kiss was hot, and she poured all of her need into it. Being with him was consuming, so potent, that she'd get married tomorrow just to do it again—if that was what he was waiting for. Because if he was waiting for her to feel ready then they were just wasting time.

Maybe he needed time?

The thought sobered her.

He stroked a fingertip along her jaw. "I lost you for a second."

She wetted her lower lip and his gaze hooked on her tongue, desire glimmering in their blue depths. "I've been wondering why we haven't...you know...since I've been here."

His arm that embraced her waist tightened. "I didn't want to rush you. You might've wanted time to get comfortable with the house first."

"You're so considerate." She'd suspected as much, but this man putting her before his needs was humbling, and more comforting that any house could be.

That was Aaron. He put everyone before his own needs. She'd lined up his boots earlier so he'd quit grabbing the wrong pair. They were already out of order, but when four guys were coming in and kicking off their footwear, jumbled was a permanent state.

Then she'd hung all the jackets and organized the hats and caps. It wasn't that she was compelled to clean up after everyone. She was bored silly.

Aaron had spent as much time with her as possible, but his work constantly called him away. A girl could only watch so much TV. Except for his mom. She watched a lot of TV.

"We'd better get going." He kissed her forehead and steered her toward the door. They grabbed their coats and boots and went out to the pickup.

Voices emanated from downstairs, but it was the TV and not his parents talking. Sometimes they argued, but it wasn't fury behind their words. They reminded her of her aunts and uncles when they all got together. They'd bug each other about tiny details until tempers rose.

Aaron's parents were kind to her, especially his dad. She might just have a soft spot for him because she missed her own terribly. Aaron had told him about Peejong's operation, and Dalisay supplemented as much information as she could.

Lori was pleasant enough. Dalisay didn't sense hostility, but she'd lose focus on the conversation or...not care if the discussion continued.

Dalisay hadn't broached the subject of asking if anything was wrong with Lori. Had his mom been that way his whole life, or had her demeanor recently changed? It was worrisome either way.

As they drove out of the yard, the snowbanks sparkled under the headlights. Only the drifts were across their path.

"The wind picked up in the last hour. It'll be fun coming home." He picked up speed on the main road. The snow hadn't piled high, but it'd puff into a cloud of flakes as he plowed through each one.

"How does a car get through this stuff?" she asked.

Aaron snorted. "It doesn't. Depends on how hard-packed it is, too, but it's either stay home until the roads are cleared or take a four-wheel drive—if you think that won't get stuck. It won't be bad enough that we can't get home. We'd probably be okay if we used Mom's car, too."

Stay home until the roads were cleared. Dalisay wouldn't be driving Aaron's truck while she was here. How was she going to get to town and back? Would she be able to drive in the summer? But Aaron said winter could be six months long. Would she be housebound all that time, or dependent on him or his brothers?

Was that why Lori had relegated herself to the basement?

Dalisay stared out the window until they reached town. Aaron cast a questioning glance her way, but probably thought she was worried about the driving conditions. And she was, but in the way of what they meant for her future.

By the time he parked in front of a plain square building surrounded by a wide parking lot, she had failed to identify how different that situation was from living on Peejong's isolated farmland. The whole reason for not moving in with him was to retain their freedom.

She didn't *feel* stifled in Moore. Not yet. But it appeared to be in her future. So did dependency on Aaron to get her around.

Aaron interrupted her thoughts, which was good. She couldn't go into the evening doubting her life here.

"Ready to meet everyone?"

She smiled and hopped out. No, she wasn't ready to meet everyone.

Aaron opened the door to the bar for her. Warm air laced with greasy food and salt wafted over her. Laughter and thumping music got louder, and she stalled. Aaron rested a hand on the small of her back. A small measure of reassurance, but it was enough to propel her forward.

They turned heads as they passed. Aaron nodded and murmured his greeting.

She whispered loud enough for him to hear, but he had to cant his head. No whisper could cover the height distance between them. "Do you know all these people?"

"Not all of them. The ones I do are more acquaintances, people I see around."

He knew someone every place they went. He might not know their name, or he might know their first name only, or just have "seen them around," but there were very few strangers to him. It was a lot like roaming her old neighborhood with her dad.

A crowd was gathered in the corner. They weren't late, but the Walkers were very punctual.

"There he is," a man yelled. A bunch of cheers erupted.

Her cheeks heated fast and hard. The pounding of her heart was planted between her ears. They were all watching her.

The hand on her back slid around to her side. She was back in her safe zone, next to him.

The next couple of hours were a whirlwind of meeting men and women with huge smiles and speculative stares. They mingled and eventually ended up at a table with Lucas and one of the cousins that Aaron worked with but wasn't part owner in the business, named Justin.

"You're Travis's brother?" she asked. She knew the answer after months of talking with Aaron and scrolling through his pictures. But Aaron and Lucas were engrossed in a conversation about the upcoming planting season and that left her and Justin looking around at all the others in their little groups.

"Yes. Aaron says you're interested in going back to school?"

She nodded. The fire she used to have for that career crept back in.

"Where would you go for the program? Are there colleges around here you can commute to?"

"I haven't checked into it much." She smiled. "Afraid to get my hopes up."

A man approached Justin, a huge grin on his face. He was striking in appearance—in a good way, but so unlike the men that she was surrounded by. And women for that matter. The top of his hair was several inches long, but the rest of his head was shaved. Thick plugs an inch wide hung in his earlobes and tattoos snaked up his muscular arms.

He patted Justin on the back. "What's up, bro? I don't see you out much." The man nodded to Aaron and Lucas. Another friend?

Justin laughed and kicked the seat out next to him. "Look who's talking. You're always on duty. Hey, maybe you can answer a question. Caleb, this is Aaron's fiancée Dalisay."

"Ah yes. News travels fast. I've heard of you." His laid-back manner made it easy to see why he fit into the Walker crowd. They were all relaxed and good-natured, giving her a case of nostalgia for her own family. She missed their get-togethers.

"You know," Caleb said to Justin, "I'm not often wanted for my brains."

"It's overrated. Dalisay was in school for nursing in the Philippines and she wants to get back into it. Where's the nearest program?"

"Dude, you know I'm a firefighter, right?"

"But you work with nurses and stuff."

Caleb cocked his head. "I date them. I don't work with them." He looked at Dalisay. "I really don't know what our local college offers, but it's a two-year school. At the most, it'd have an LPN program if it has anything, but not a four-year degree."

She refused to let her hopes crash. There had to be other places around.

Caleb continued. "They have a paramedic training program, a peace officer program, and a fire academy, but I didn't hear of nursing while I was there. Check it out, though. It's been years since I've gone through the academy."

"Where are the closest universities?" She tried recalling all the research she'd done, but it'd been a long night—good, but long. Her brain was full of new information on people's names and faces. And after her moment of doubt earlier, this wasn't helping.

"Universities?" Justin answered. "Sioux Falls is a two-hour drive. Moorhead with Fargo across the river is a healthy hour drive. The other towns around us are too small, they'd have community colleges."

Oh. She forced a smile. "Thanks. I'll check on it."

Caleb scanned the bar like he was looking for someone. "You can always commute. The drive in the winter sucks. I've been called to enough accidents to know it's not something I'd do." He looked at Justin. "I'm gonna go to the bar to order. Your brother's table is hogging Trina."

Justin winced. "It's probably my sister's pretentious new boyfriend, asking for the wine list or some shit."

"Then I'm out. I have a hard enough time with her." He slid off his chair. "Want something?"

Justin stood, too. "I'll come with. I need a refill or two. Talk to you later, Dalisay."

Aaron and Lucas were engrossed in a who's planting what this year discussion. She tapped Aaron's arm. "I'm going to the comfort room, uh, restroom."

She left them there. In the bathroom, she did her business and soaked in the calmer atmosphere of the comfort room. Bathroom. She had to get used to calling it a bathroom or no one would know what she was talking about. The door opened and closed a few times, but Dalisay had to gather herself a few more minutes.

In university when she'd gone out to party, she'd never been this overwhelmed before. Neither had she been when she met her ex's parents and siblings. His aunts and uncles had outnumbered the Walkers, but this was different. She couldn't explain how.

She blew out a slow breath and exited the stall. One of the women she'd seen running around taking orders and delivering drinks was adjusting her ponytail at the counter. She met Dalisay's gaze in the mirror.

"So you're the one Aaron got to marry into the crazy."

The crazy what? Nothing about Aaron's life was wild. The basset hound that ignored her and everyone else certainly wasn't. Half-tamed barn cats could claim the title.

"I'm his fiancée, yes." Dalisay scooted around her to wash her hands. In the mirror, she made out the woman's nametag. What a surprise. Trina. Defensiveness lined her spine. "And I don't think his family's crazy."

Trina raised her brows like she knew better. "They might be hiding it until it's too late. I wasn't surprised he had to go so far away from home to find someone." Her smile turned smug. "We used to date. He wanted more, but I turned him down."

Dalisay inhaled a measured breath. She wasn't a fighter, nor was she nasty. But her parents raised her to think for herself and go after her goals. She was in America because she was going after what she wanted and happened to find a man she desired to spend her life with along the way.

School and the commute were bothering her enough. Another woman tampering with her relationship? There was enough to deal with.

She dried her hands and spoke as clearly as possible. She

wouldn't let her accent be another reason for Trina to think she was better. "You met his parents?"

Trina's expression turned guarded. "No."

"You've met his brothers?"

"Nick and Jake—Jackson." She clenched her jaw. "No, I haven't met them."

"He prefers Nicolas. They're very polite young men. They each take a night and cook. Did you know that?"

Trina's eyes narrowed. She was on to what Dalisay was doing. Good.

"I don't understand why you've judged them if you haven't even met them." Dalisay stepped around Trina toward the door.

"Be careful. Or the Walkers will control your life so much, you'll end up unhappy, with no skills, that you have to move back in with your grown child and do nothing with your life."

Ouch. That hit close to home. But it wasn't in Dalisay's nature to cower. To be shy—yes. Meek? Often. To be a coward —not today. "Lori Walker has raised a man who runs a sizable business and cares for his family. I'll be proud to call Nicolas and Jackson brothers. And before you target his dad, I'll let you know that Aaron can't get him to quit working in his retirement. Now, if you'll excuse me, I have to get back to *my family*."

She slipped out the door, refusing to make a scene.

She almost ran into Aaron, who grabbed her by the shoulders. "I was just coming to make sure you found your way all right. What was I thinking? How could you get lost in a small-town bar when you used to navigate Manila at night?"

Trina stormed past them, her head down.

Aaron paled. "Did something happen?"

Someone else left the bathroom, but Dalisay didn't look.

A woman guffawed. "I'll say something happened. That was a solid burn on Trina."

Abbi waddled by, her pregnant belly on display with a shirt that said "Time To Pop." She nailed Aaron in the shoulder with a fist. "She's like your dog's gas. Quiet, but deadly."

Abbi disappeared around the corner and Aaron raised a brow. "Wanna tell me what that's all about?"

That she couldn't take any more insecurity about how this marriage was going to work? No. "If I don't show that I take our relationship seriously, no one else will. I'll just say that Trina will now, too."

He grinned. "Good. She can play her games with someone else." His gaze dipped to her mouth. "Wanna head home?"

# CHAPTER 15

hey bounded through the snow and into the house. Aaron shuttled Daisy in first and quietly shut the door behind them. Seeing her go from bashful, nerve-ridden fiancée to ferocious, overprotective, and ready to throw down had him tied in knots.

She'd talked to him about her possessive streak and how it had only gotten worse after her ex's unfaithfulness. Aaron wasn't ashamed to admit that he relished it. Was that bad? After so many years of women fleeing from him, using him only for a good time, he was engaged to a woman who'd stand up for not only him, but his entire hot mess of a family.

As if she sensed him thinking about her, she glanced at him over her shoulder as she hung her coat up. He was going to toss his on the floor, but he made the extra effort to be tidy. It'd become such a habit, he'd have to consciously work to break it, and point out to the others how they'd let things slide.

Her expression was as steeped in primal need as his. The last week of keeping his hands to himself had been a special form of hell. Worse were the constant questions: Did she want him again? Would she ever be comfortable enough to have sex under the same roof as his parents? They hadn't done more than hold hands around Mari.

Her gaze strayed to the entrance of the basement.

He grabbed her hand and they tiptoed past the opening. Nothing but the TV emanated from downstairs.

Daisy suppressed a giggle and they darted around the corner, past the kitchen, to the hallway. She stopped, and he bumped into her.

"What's wrong?" he whispered. He hadn't snuck a girl into his house—ever. But this felt like a whispering moment. The last thing he wanted to do was ruin the mood.

"Which bedroom are we going to?"

He crept closer to her and pushed her hair behind one ear. "I want to be with you in our bed." What if she wanted to wait until they were officially married? "That is, unless you want to wait. I mean we just—"

She towed him toward her door. Thank goodness. He would've waited, willingly, as happily as he could've, but his body was primed for her. The silk of her skin, her breathy moans—he would've resorted to cold showers.

The second they crossed into the room, he butted the door shut and swept her into his arms. Their mouths clashes, and their hands fumbled with shirts. She deftly undid the buttons on his shirt and shoved it down his shoulders. He abandoned his attempt to lift the hem of her long sweater and shrugged his top off the rest of the way.

She whipped her own shirt off.

His breath gusted out. "Aw, now that's a sight I've been wanting to see."

Her greedy gaze drank him in. "Same here."

They each fiddled with their own pants until they were shed. He couldn't wait for her to take off her underclothes.

His mouth was back on hers and she was in his arms with

her hands in his hair, and her legs wrapping around him. His cock was cocooned between them and for now, it was almost content. She was going to be his again.

The bed hit the back of his legs and he plopped down. Scooting back, he held her to him.

He laid down. The vision before him was staggering. Her hair was draped over both shoulders, her legs straddling him, her eyes full of desire and promise.

"I wish I could tell you how beautiful you are."

She trailed a finger down to his navel. "You do. In so many ways. You make me feel special." She blinked like it was a realization. "I can't believe we found each other."

He caught her hand and nibbled on her palm. "But we did. I'll find you wherever you are."

A sly smile curved her lips. She tilted her head, and her smile faltered. "Tonight was…nice."

"Next time will be more fun, I promise. Fewer people and less chaotic. And I'll try not to talk shop with Lucas all night."

She unhooked her bra. His erection twitched in anticipation. "I like watching you talk farming."

The bra slipped off and dangled in her hand. He hardly noticed, his gaze riveted to her pert breasts. He skimmed his hands up her sides to cup one in each hand. Lush, warm, a balm to the part of him that had stressed over being separated from her.

She leaned over him, her hands landing on each side of his head. Her hair hung over them like a privacy curtain. Her position was the only thing that could coax his hands off her breasts. He threaded his fingers under the waist of her panties and she helped him get them off.

Her hot sex landed on his straining cock. He groaned. She rocked and closed the gap between them to kiss them.

With one hand, he fumbled for the drawer handle. He'd stocked the end table with condoms, hoping he wasn't being too presumptuous, but dreading an interruption of any kind if he was fortunate to be with her.

She stilled, her mouth frowning against him.

"Condom," he said against her lips. They hadn't had the "do you want kids" talk yet, other than to say they each wanted kids. The process of getting married loomed before them and it was unspoken that they wanted to wait until they cleared that hurdle before broaching the topic of when and how many.

Her pelvis rubbed against his and another moan escaped. He'd come if she did that again. Skin on skin. The sensation was unparalleled, just like the angle with him.

He rolled the condom on before she offered to do it. Same fear of climaxing too soon.

Moving her hands to his chest, she used him for leverage to lift herself onto him.

"Don't you need me to— Ohhhh." No. She was wet and eager for him.

How'd he get so lucky with his flower?

Daisy forced her lungs to fill as she seated herself over Aaron's shaft. From this angle, she needed to adjust for his size.

She rocked her hips, and they both hissed. Her belly clenched. She wanted to relish the experience. They'd have more, but this was their first time in months and it was gooood.

She'd been ready to sink onto him without protection. Glad he was thinking clearer. As much as she wanted to be a mom, she wanted time with her man. Time to be a wife, time to settle into the country, time to learn who Daisy Walker was as Dalisay Calamba Cortez slipped into her subconscious.

Sliding up, she paused and met his gaze. His lips were parted, like hers, his knees braced behind her. The descent onto him was bliss. Her walls pulsed around him so hard her abdominal muscles were going to be sore.

"Aaron," she gasped.

"I'm here, my flower. Just don't stop."

Rocking up, she did as he asked and rode him. His hands were all over her, his rough fingertips setting nerve endings on fire. He palmed a breast in each hand and she slammed her hands over his. She dropped her head back and picked up the pace.

His breathing quickened, as did hers. Coiling tighter and tighter deep inside, the erotic pressure built. She didn't want it to end, wanted to ride the precipice. She wanted the validation that this was real—and was going to last.

His grunts mingled with her moans. She bit her lower lip to keep herself quiet. Her ass slapped against his thighs, and he crunched his torso up as he ground into her. His erection thickened and, oh god, that was all she could take.

With the quietest shout she could manage, she turned herself over to her orgasm. Her body shook in Aaron's grip. He shuddered underneath her, gritting her name between his teeth. Her pleasure continued until Aaron sprawled flat. She collapsed onto him.

His chest rose and fell, but he welcomed her, his arms clasping her against him.

"I think we both needed that," he murmured in her ear.

She giggled and stroked his chest. Yes to the release, but a resounding yes to being intimate with him.

He adjusted her until she was cozied underneath a blanket, then disappeared for a minute to dispose of the condom.

When he curled back around her, she fully relaxed for the first time since she'd arrived.

"What's it going to be like?" she asked.

"What do you mean?" His voice rumbled through her back. The night before he'd left Manila, they'd talked like this. It flew to the top of her favorite things to do list.

"Our wedding? You said we'd go to the courthouse and have a big celebration after."

He swirled lazy circles with his finger on her hip. "It's your wedding, too. So…whatever you want it to be like."

She smiled, grateful he was behind her and couldn't see how it must be laced with sadness. Ina.

"I mean, you pick the dress you want. As fancy or as plain as you want. We'll pick music to dance to that we both like, and if you meet anyone in town that you want to invite, you know you don't have to ask me."

"When is it going to happen?" Part of her wanted it to happen now. The other part whispered that there was no rush. Other than the time limit before her visa expired, she was here, Aaron was here, and all was well.

"I'll be honest, I would marry you tomorrow. But to have the reception with semi-decent weather, the dance hall had an opening that I booked at the end of March. We can change it, but it would also be at the start of planting season. Any later and I'll be in the fields, any earlier and we risk a spring blizzard canceling everything."

About a month and a half from now. "And until then? What do I do?"

"Whatever you want. Look at nursing programs and decide where you want to go."

Her world dimmed a few shades. "I…don't know if that'll work out like I thought." She told him about her conversation with Justin and Caleb.

He stroked her arm. "We'll figure something out."

She didn't reply. The information had sunk harder than she'd thought.

He nudged her until she rolled to face him. Tears burned the back of her eyes. Despite her own internal warnings, she'd gotten her hopes up about going back to school.

Ina had moved her old textbooks to the home she was working in. Dalisay had almost packed them whether they were useless in her new curriculum or not.

Only now there wouldn't be any more school.

She blinked hard to keep tears from gathering in her eyes. It wasn't Aaron's problem. He had his own job; he supported so many others. He didn't need to worry about her.

She forced a smile. "I can check it out while you're working. If you don't mind me using your computer."

"What's mine is yours."

He was growing hard between them again. Her gaze dipped down, not that she could see anything in the dark.

He flipped her to her back and spread out over her. "I know I need to be heading back to my own room soon, but… We have time, right?"

She shouldn't care whether his parents knew they were sleeping together already. They were adults. But she was the one hanging around them all day. The girl he'd brought to America. Aaron never pushed it. He sensed her desire for discretion.

She cradled him between her legs. She'd take as much time with him as she could.

# CHAPTER 16

*D*alisay crossed her legs on the couch and faced out the four-pane picture window. Snow fell, the flakes in spiky clusters. There was an inch on the ground and it was supposed to be on and off flurries all day.

Then the wind was supposed to pick up.

The end of February sucked as bad as the beginning of the month.

She pressed her lips together and forced herself back to the conversation with Ina. The time difference and Ina's schedule interfered with planning calls, but really, it was all around Ina's schedule. Because Dalisay certainly had nothing going on.

Ina chattered about the latest house gossip. The couple she worked for had met like Dalisay and Aaron. The wife was a few years older than her and the husband was an expat of the United States and about the age of Aaron's dad.

"What does she do all day?" Dalisay asked.

Ina clucked. "She raises the kids. Believe me, they give her enough to do."

Dalisay smiled. At times like this she could see the appeal

of immediately starting a family, just for the benefit that'd she'd have something to do and someone to talk to. Then she'd be well on her journey of turning into her aunt.

Aaron was gone all day. He worked in his shop, he was on the road hauling grain or equipment. Cash would call, needing help with the cattle now that he had a newborn baby boy to attend to. Abbi was recovering fine, but Dalisay hardly saw her.

She'd hear Aaron and his dad talk. Abbi had Elle or Kami to help her out. Brock's wife was friendly and always willing to lend a hand, but the couple kept a low profile. Josie wasn't one to call and invite her over. And Dalisay didn't know any of them well enough to beg them to come visit.

Beg. She was ready to.

Aaron's brothers managed to never be home, but Dalisay hadn't left the house for an entire week.

*Don't worry. I picked up groceries while I was in town.*

*Yeah, the roads are icy, but spring's around the corner.*

*I did the dishes before I left so you don't have to.*

She did laundry and straightened the mudroom. Aaron bugged the others to help. Nice gesture, but she nearly told him to shut his mouth.

Nicolas and Jackson had their cooking nights. She dominated the other evenings, learning to cook some of their favorites. Once in a while, she'd venture down to ask Lori questions about recipes—and make sure she was still alive.

Ina could run, swim, and bike circles around Lori, and it was sad. They were about the same age, but the life behind Lori's eyes was that of an eighty year old.

No, that wasn't correct, either. Agnes, Aaron's grandma was livelier than Lori, too. Dalisay had met her last weekend. Her one and only outing in the last two weeks.

The visit had been...good. Agnes was polite, curious, and couldn't say her name at all. She'd asked several questions about Dalisay and her family, and then had trapped Aaron for an hour talking about the farm and planting plans for the spring.

Dalisay had tried not to zone out. Her phone had been a siren call to mindlessly scroll through it while Aaron and his grandma were engrossed in soybeans versus canola. She hadn't wanted to be rude, and had sat and listened while suppressing her yawn.

"Dali," Ina cut in. "Did you hear me?"

"Sorry. What'd you say?"

"I asked how it was really going. Each time I call, you're less and less excited. Today, you're nearly despondent."

She'd picked up on it? It wouldn't do to have Ina worry about her. "It's the weather. I like the snow, but it's so limiting."

"For everyone, or just you?"

Of all the times to be astute. "I can't drive yet, and if I did, I don't have a vehicle." She could use Lori's car, but no license. "Then I'd have to brave the roads. They're all used to it."

Ina scoffed. "People move to wintery climates all the time. Don't let that scare you." She sighed. "You're not happy."

"No, I am." Dalisay watched the flakes pile on the windowsill. "It's not what I thought."

"Moore isn't, or Aaron isn't?"

"Moore." Aaron was all she could've imagined. What she saw of him other than an hour of cuddling and watching TV, or more, at night before he'd sneak back to his own room.

"It's not much better than staying with Peejong and marrying Michael." Ina's frank tone nailed it perfectly.

"At Peejong's I'd have something to do," she mumbled.

This so wasn't Manila. And that was okay. She didn't have to worry about the geese migrating back north mugging her. But she'd lived in Manila for five years and had grown accustomed to her freedom. Freedom to go anywhere by many means of transit. Freedom to grab a cup of coffee—on any corner. Freedom to get out and walk around.

The half-tame barn cats were getting used to her presence, but they weren't the best conversationalists. She'd worked at a busy internet café where she chatted with coworkers, learned about the life of some of her regulars, and talked to people.

This house. It was so quiet.

"You'll find your way." Ina's encouragement wasn't surprising. She didn't expect Dalisay to give up easily. "I know you can make it work. It's what we do."

"They don't have nursing school here." Dalisay squeezed her eyes shut. She hadn't planned to spill that to her mom.

Ina would probably say what Aaron had. *We'll check it out. We'll find something.* Meanwhile, he hadn't mentioned a thing about it and she'd gotten frustrated with her research. There were no options that didn't involve travel, and she couldn't even get to town to buy a coffee.

And she didn't like coffee!

The familiar burn of tears returned. She hadn't broken down yet, and she wasn't going to today.

"There's nothing?" Ina sounded genuinely disturbed. She'd always been Dalisay's biggest supporter. She had gushed to relatives how her daughter was going to work in the city at a big hospital.

Dalisay hadn't even walked past a major hospital in years. Not very nurse-like.

"All of it is a commute. And while the time of travel might be the same as in Manila, the distance isn't. Neither is the weather. I don't think it's going to happen."

"What does the college in town offer?"

"Two-year degrees, like in farm management and accounting."

"Well, there you go."

To Ina it was simple. Pivot. Plan one thing, life throws a different option. Dalisay needed to be more like her.

"Maybe I should look into them." She lacked conviction.

"You'd be more satisfied."

Yeah. Maybe.

An engine approached. Dalisay craned her neck to look toward the driveway, her heart skipping a beat. Was Aaron returning from Brock's early?

Jackson drove by.

"I need to go, Dali. Hang in there. You can make this work. You owe it to yourself and to Aaron."

The feeling of failure wasn't helping anything. If it weren't for getting exposed to the light of day thanks to the windows, and the occasional foray to wander around the yard, she might as well curl in a blanket in the basement and watch daytime TV with Lori.

She clicked off the phone and stared out the window.

This place was gorgeous with its blanket of white. Between snowfalls, the banks and piles melted enough to reveal the dirty brown snow underneath, but somehow it managed to maintain a sense of tranquility. An understanding to slow down because as long as it's there, there's not much that can be done.

A concept that hit home more for Dalisay every day.

Her phone buzzed. Aaron!

"I'm gonna be at Cash's a little longer. Dad and I are moving snow so he won't have to worry about it."

"How's little Carter?" She would've like to have gone with Aaron, but while he and Timothy worked, she would've hovered over a new mama, wondering if she'd worn out her welcome an hour ago.

"Cute as can be. Abbi's napping and Cash is passed out in the recliner with Carter passed out on his chest. I guess the baby hardly sleeps at night. So don't wait to eat or anything. I can make something for me and Dad when we get back."

Always courteous. Always taking care of everyone else. She'd wanted a career where she could do that, but she couldn't even do it in her own home.

Home. Squaring her shoulders, she said goodbye to Aaron and stood.

She owed it to herself to make this her home. This would be her first meal without Aaron. Only Jackson and Lori were here, but she could take care of them so Aaron didn't have to worry.

Determination infused her movements. Time for dinner.

DALISAY JUMPED when Lori came upstairs. She'd announced that the meal was ready *fifteen* minutes ago.

The food was cooling and her plate was empty. She'd spent much of the time wondering if she should serve herself and get started, or if that'd be considered rude.

Lori sat. Her pale face was creased like she'd just woken from a dead sleep smashed into a pillow. "Oh. Pork chops. And rice again. I see you're really getting use out of the rice cooker Aaron bought."

"Yes, that was very considerate." She had rice with her meals everyday even if the Walkers didn't. Each batch, she added extra. The potatoes that the others made were good, but a taste of home each day helped her adjust.

Lori dished her plate, not waiting for Jackson who may have muttered something about grabbing a bite in town. Dalisay served herself and they ate quietly.

Did she try to make conversation again? She barely knew Lori well enough to ask her about anything.

"It's going to be quiet with Jackson gone next year." She

could kick herself, but it was something. This woman was supposed to become family, but she knew some of her café clients better than Lori.

Lori's small smile didn't reach her eyes. "Time flies. One day they're babies, the next they're going off to college. I never would've thought…"

Dalisay waited with her fork poised over her plate. Should she prompt her?

But Lori finished. "He was such a challenging kid. Nicolas, too. Each in their own way, but so unlike Aaron." Lori shrugged, and she sliced her pork chop. "Maybe it's the age difference. Aaron was an only child for so long. And he was an easy kid." Her smile this time was real. "Then the boys came one right after the other. I had them, and Aaron's football games, chores around here. Then, oh god, baseball. Practice every night. Games were double headers and I had to suffer through them with two toddlers who wanted to eat sunflower seed shells off the floor—other people's."

She fell quiet again, her expression growing tired.

"Sounds like a challenging time," Dalisay said. This brief glimpse into Lori said so much. The way Aaron's mom acted had felt personal, but this conversation was promising. Lori wasn't resentful that Aaron was getting married or that he had met his fiancée online.

"It was. It can still be. Both the younger boys were in football and baseball, too, like Aaron. You know, small towns."

She didn't. Solano was five times the size of Moore.

"Jackson quit playing before high school. It was the ol' playtime is based on the merits of your coach's drinking buddies and their kids, and of course, who donated the most to the program. Jackson's like me, doesn't put up with the bullshit. Nicolas starts baseball again this spring. He can drive himself to practice now. I'll still have to go to games, I suppose. Then it's one more year of football to suffer through."

Dalisay's face must've registered surprise. Lori elaborated. "I worry about head injuries with everything in the news, but the biggest drama are the other parents. If you don't play their way, your kid doesn't play." She waved her hand like she was shooing the topic away. "Anyway, I'm sure it'll be different when you and Aaron have kids. Jackson tells me you were looking for nursing programs."

The subject changed to one that was depressing, but Lori had broached it and that was more than Dalisay expected this morning. So there was a silver lining.

"I may have to change plans. There's nothing close by."

"I imagine the thought of commuting when you have so much going on is a bit daunting."

That part wasn't a problem. Dalisay had nothing going on. Her troubles were not having a car or license.

She nodded instead of mentioning any of that. "Ina—my mother—said I should look at the other programs the school offers."

"It's not the same, though, is it?"

Dalisay popped her gaze up. The look of complete understanding staggered her. Had Lori made the same decision at one time?

Lori inclined her head as if affirming her mental question. "I loved fashion, design—anything with fabric, I was all over it. But I met Timothy. You can guess that Moore doesn't offer much in the way of fashion design or home interior training. I went to the college in town, then got my four-year degree online. Business." She shrugged. "It helped the farm."

Dalisay's gaze strayed to the living room. The furniture matched and was nice enough. The pictures on the wall were outdoorsy, but nothing about the place screamed *I love decorating*.

Lori chuckled. "This is Aaron's haphazard style. I didn't want to touch it when I moved back." She sighed. "This house isn't mine."

Yeah. Dalisay knew the feeling. It was supposed to become hers, but her suitcase wasn't even fully unpacked.

"If you…" Lori pushed her rice around. "If you decide to change it up in here, let me know if you want some ideas. I'd show you pictures of how I had it when I lived here, but the style's outdated by a good twenty years."

"Yes, I'd like that." Her answer seemed to please Lori. She even ate some food. But it depressed Dalisay more. Was this her future? Living in a house that really wasn't hers, buried under lost hopes and dreams?

*a*aron shut the door to the pickup. His dad climbed out, too. The shop was quiet and a nice break from working in the wind. They'd moved snow the weekend before to help Cash out, then he and his cousins worked on clearing their own property and road. The one that ran past all their places wasn't an emergency route, and the county had gotten spoiled with how well the Walkers cared for it that they never rushed after a significant snowfall.

"I keep expecting Dalisay to open up, but she's still so quiet." Dad went around to the rear of the pickup and dropped the tailgate. He started unloading the supplies they'd picked up from town.

There'd been a sale on landscape rock. Once the snow melted, the sad state of the flower beds and decorative stone would be glaring. A few more bags of river rock would bring it to life. Fingers crossed that the long-neglected flowers returned.

"She's shy around you guys, that's all. She talks more around her own family, but overall, she has a calm personality." Aaron hoped Dad didn't notice that he was worried as well.

Daisy was quieter than usual. Most of the nights this past week, she'd said she was tired and going to sleep. He got no invite to her room and she hadn't asked to visit his.

Last night, he'd taken the night off to plan their reception. The dance hall was booked, the DJ, the music picked out, but he wanted more of her input. Getting her opinions on any of it was like pulling a milk bottle away from a calf. She was fighting to keep it to herself.

Conversations were one-sided and her answers monosyllabic until it was like talking to his mom.

The thought stopped him in his tracks. The thump of bags of rock stacking on the pallet kept going without him. Damn, he had to help Dad before the man threw his back out. Though, he didn't think anything would slow his dad down. He was the most active retiree in the tristate area.

Aaron hauled the bags of supplies out. He and Dad had inventoried tools and replaced all the ones that had broken or weakened over the winter. This weekend, they planned to tackle the machinery that'd be used heavily in the summer, like the lawn mower. The duties were pretty minor. Necessary, but not critical.

"Dad, do you mind if I take the rest of the day off? I'm getting married in a few weeks and I haven't spent much time with my fiancée lately."

"Date night?"

"Date weekend? We can pry Nicolas away from his girlfriend to help you out."

Dad grunted. "Good luck with that. Jackson's in town picking out his tux. Prom's over a month away, but you know him. Always prepared."

"Then I'll finish up—"

"Aaron." Dad rested an arm on the box of the pickup and

propped his other hand on his hip. "I was changing oil in lawn mowers before I could drive. I can handle it. Go get Daisy out of the house. It's finally above thirty degrees today. I don't know anyone who wouldn't be stricken with a serious case of cabin fever. Well, except your mother."

"Right?" When had he last run to town with Daisy?

Was that what was going on, she was going stir crazy?

Aaron jogged to the house. It was early afternoon on a Saturday. What was there to do in Moore?

He trotted into the house and kicked off his boots and coat. Before spinning around the corner, he ducked back and lined his boots up and hung up his coat. His siblings had been making an effort after seeing Daisy taking some care in the mudroom.

Padding through the house, he heard nothing but the TV from downstairs. Once he cleared the kitchen and dining room, he spotted her. She was cross-legged on the couch, her head resting in one hand while she gazed out the window. His laptop was open in her lap, but the screen had blacked out.

Yeah, something was going on.

"Daisy?"

She jerked her head up. "I didn't hear you come in." Her hands were sucked into the sleeves of her sweater, leaving only her fingers out.

"If you're cold, you can turn up the heat."

"No, I'm fine." She closed the computer and placed it on the floor. Then she stood and stretched. He tracked the movement of her lithe body. It'd been too long since he'd seen it. Her winter clothing swallowed her up. "Did you forget something?"

He grinned. "Nope. I'm taking the rest of the day off. Tomorrow, too."

Her eyes brightened. "To do what?"

"Want to go to town and see a movie?"

"Yes," she breathed. "I'll go get ready." And she was gone to her room.

He peeked out the window to where she had been staring. The driveway. Must be cabin fever bothering her.

His brothers were in town. Mom was downstairs. Otherwise the house was the quietest he'd heard it. When he was home, he was always banging around and doing stuff. Daisy had nothing to do.

He'd have to ask her about that. All his efforts to relieve pressure for her might have left her bereft.

She reappeared just as quietly as she left. Her hair was pulled back and she looked refreshed.

THEY'D BEEN in town for hours. Daisy had opened up more, but she still wasn't as talkative as she had been when they'd been able to escape alone together.

Aaron pulled into the restaurant's parking lot. It was full, but then, it was Saturday night. He hadn't been out for a real Saturday night date in years. This place didn't have a band or dancing, it was for eating only. He was being both selfish and cautious—they needed to talk.

The hostess seated them in a booth. Aaron nodded to a few people he knew, but none were close friends. They may have heard he was engaged, but wouldn't have spared Daisy any attention.

Of course, her being new to town would garner plenty of attention. He hoped she wasn't offended. The truth was, if they hadn't met, he'd have ogled with each step she took. She was striking, sexy, and her mellow attitude made her seem attainable.

Daisy cruised the menu and asked for recommendations.

She settled on a simple sirloin despite him pushing the filet mignon. The price difference scared her off. He ordered sirloin tips and settled back.

"So, want to tell me what's going on?" He kept any lightness out of his voice. His question was serious.

"I'm sorry?" She fiddled with her napkin, stretching it out, folding it, straightening it again, and rolling it around her finger.

"I feel like the longer you're here, the more miserable you are."

"I'm not miserable."

Where was the passion?

"Yes, you are."

She shook her head, her eyes full of determination. "I'm not. You have a wonderful house and your family is pleasant."

Not exactly resounding compliments. He switched tactics. "What about college? What have you found out?"

Her expression shut down. It wasn't blank, but it was guarded. "Nothing really. I've been researching the programs offered by MCC."

She was calling Moore Community College by its acronym. That had to be a good sign. Like a form of acceptance, right?

"What program are you interested in?"

"Um… Probably accounting, or something."

Aaron clenched his jaw. Could her tone have been any deader? She wasn't being honest with him. He asked as much as he could think of about MCC and she answered. No enthusiasm sparked in her eyes.

Their meal arrived, and Daisy's eyes widened. "That's a lot of food."

"The dog likes leftovers. Or you can get a to-go box and have the rest tomorrow."

He waited for her reaction over the food. Because of the

weather and getting wrapped up in work, this was her first night out. She'd been in Moore for over a month and he hadn't taken her on a proper date.

"We'll go out again, tomorrow," he blurted. "And get dessert tonight."

She raised her brows at his sudden demands. "Okay?"

He grinned. "Okay."

She giggled. The tension drained between them and the discussion transitioned to the major decision of cheesecake or fudge brownie with ice cream.

They finished dinner and strolled out into the chilly night air.

Daisy stuffed her hands in her coat pocket. "I can tell it's warming up."

"Spring is one of my favorite seasons." He wrapped an arm around her. "The air is fresh and doesn't give you a brain freeze. The snow melts and we can drive normally again. Plants grow. The landscape turns green. The days are warmer, and I don't have to wear so many layers." He chuckled. "Like I said, it's my favorite."

"I look forward to it."

He helped her into the cab. As he was climbing in the driver's side, his phone rang.

"Hey, Justin," he answered.

"Aaron, can you work the sheep tomorrow—and for the next few days? I have to tie up some loose ends in Denver. My old boss is losing her shit that I left an account hanging when I quit."

"No problem. Text me a list of what needs to be done."

He stuffed his phone back in his pocket. "Justin needs to leave town. I'm gonna be a sheep guy for a few days."

"So you'll be working tomorrow?"

He looked at her. She wasn't facing him, but her profile

spoke volumes. Pursed lips, tight jaw, rampant disappointment in her expression.

"It won't take long to feed the sheep. I'll have to check on whether any are lambing. We've only had sheep for a little over a year and we're still learning what to expect."

"Okay."

He jabbered about their flock of sheep. Daisy murmured bland responses.

He'd announced that he planned to spend the weekend with her and as soon as Justin called, he'd shifted his priorities.

Pulling into his yard, he asked, "Are you upset that I'm helping Justin out tomorrow?"

"No. You need to be there for him. I understand."

There was the lack of conviction again. Not so much lack of conviction, but like he'd let her down, and she understood, but she was tired of understanding.

If his work hours were too much after a month, how was she going to handle years? Long days of planting, full nights of harvest, then winter hauls, not to mention covering cattle and sheep duties.

Had he been mistaken? Was there no woman willing to deal with both him and his chosen career?

The pickup door opened, and Daisy slipped out.

He scrambled out and jogged after her. "Talk to me."

"We've been talking all night, Aaron."

He stopped, and she kept going. Her slight weight making little sound on the snow packed gravel. Instead of calling for her, he crossed to the edge of the driveway and grabbed a handful of snow. Packing it into a light snowball, he squinted after Daisy. She hadn't looked back.

He took aim. His throw was gentle, and his target was the middle of her back.

The toss was off. It thumped her ass and disintegrated into a shower of icy flakes.

She gasped, her hands flying to the snow imprinted on her butt cheek.

He laughed and snatched another handful of snow. His gloves were stuffed in his pockets, but he had a few snowballs to make before he lost feeling in his fingers.

"Did you just…" She narrowed her eyes on him.

He threw the next one as gently as he could. She sidestepped and rushed to her own pile of snow. Like him, she wasn't wearing gloves, but she didn't let it stop her.

He let her throw her snowball before he formed another and tossed it. Hers landed at his boots. His hit her shoulder and it sprayed across her face. Her mouth dropped open in an indignant hiss.

"I've had more practice." He was mid laugh when she scooped a heap of snow in both hands and sprinted toward him. She chucked it in his face.

It clogged his mouth and plastered against his eyes. He coughed and spit snow chunks to the ground.

"Oh no!" She giggled, but there was concern. "Are you okay?"

"Not yet." He charged her.

She shrieked and spun, but she only got a few steps. He wrapped his arms around her tiny waist and dove into a snow drift.

They landed with an oomph. He rolled so she was on top and out of the worst of the cold.

She was laughing and trying to catch her breath.

He loved seeing her have fun and come alive after the last couple weeks of melancholy.

"You gonna talk to me yet?" She stilled, her wet hair draped across his chest. "It's me working. That's the problem, isn't it?"

She shook her head and raised her gaze. "I'm frustrated because…" She looked away. "Because…I'm bored. You take care of everybody and that leaves nothing for anybody to do."

Her brows were still furrowed. Shouldn't she look relieved?

"And?" he pressed.

"And I'm not used to being so confined." Now her expression relaxed.

So that was it. She was like a prisoner in his house. And while she said there was nothing for her to do, she certainly didn't mean she wanted more housework. She could demand to do it all, but each one of them had to pull their own weight. Going outside was even hard for her.

"It won't be like this forever." She dragged her gaze back to his and he kept going. "We'll work on getting your license and as soon as you get one, I'll have a car waiting for you." He hugged her close, willing to tolerate the cold seeping into his back and melting through his clothing a few moments longer. "Just bear with me. I know this part sucks for you."

She patted his chest. Under the yard lights, the redness in her hands was apparent. "This part doesn't suck. I'm sorry I was…" She exhaled.

"Pensive? Solemn? A grumpy Gus?"

"A what?"

"What we call a grump person. And I'm sorry it took me so long to catch on." He hugged her tight and jumped up. "I need to get you inside and warm you up. I have the perfect way to do it."

Her grin turned sultry. "Race you." She sprung away from him and he grinned, counting to five before sprinting after her.

# CHAPTER 18

*D*aisy pried an eyelid open. It was horribly early, but Aaron was nudging her shoulder.

"You don't have to come if you don't want to," he said in a hushed voice.

That's right. He'd persuaded her to tag along for chores. And she'd agreed because if he was getting up early to feed the sheep, then he could sleep over in her bedroom. They were getting married soon, yet she was still hesitant to let his family see them together.

They'd all been home and in their own rooms last night. Aaron had closed his temporary bedroom door and slept beside her the rest of the night. After an orgasm or three.

She'd rather be tucked into his side than getting ready for working in the cold, but it was that or spend the day cruising TV.

Groaning, she slid out from between the cozy covers. She was grabbing what she'd worn the night before from where it was strewn around the room. Aaron turned on the lamp. Blinking against the dim light, she squinted at him.

He was already dressed and looking too delectable this early.

"You might want to wear some clothes you don't mind getting dirty. Unless you want to wait in the truck; that's fine, too."

Hanging out in the pickup didn't sound like a blast. She nodded.

She was about to go looking through her meager stash when he interrupted her again. "I'll pull the truck up to the house. Meet me in ten?"

Ten. Like minutes? But she'd just crawled out of bed. So had he, though.

"I eat breakfast on the go. I'll grab you something. You might want to get into your snow pants, too." His departing smile was almost apologetic.

She didn't want to slow his day down. What to wear for sheep?

She chose a pair of leggings her snow pants would slide over. Throwing on a T-shirt, she shivered. A sweater, too.

In the bathroom, she combed her hair back, twisted it into a bun, and secured it. If Uncle Peejong could see her now. Dalisay, working sheep when she had refused to move in with him.

Headlights from the pickup glowed through the living room window. Billows of exhaust curled and floated around the vehicle. Since the Walkers kept their equipment running well, it must be frigid out.

She donned all her winter gear and rushed outside. Other than the chuff of the engine, there was no other sound. She was used to stepping out the door to a variety of noises. Engines, honks, people. With Peejong, or even in Solano, there were still others moving around and local wildfire.

When it was this cold in Moore, Minnesota, not even birds chirped.

She crawled into the cab. Empty. In the mirrors, Aaron's lanky form, bulked up from the coveralls, crossed from the barn.

He climbed in and smiled. "Sorry, I was feeding the cats. Pop-Tart?" A silver foil packet sat on the dash in front of her. A water bottle full of orange juice was in her cup holder.

He'd gotten breakfast for them both and fed the animals? The only tasks she'd crossed off her list were "go to the comfort room" and "get dressed."

"Thank you." The food was possible to eat without taking her gloves off.

He drove out of the yard and around the corner. She quit chewing when he turned into the driveway neighboring his.

"I know it seems crazy to drive next door," Aaron said as he parked by the house. "But the walk is almost half a mile. And I don't think we want to stroll in these temperatures."

She shook her head. Definitely not. The inside of the cab hadn't warmed yet, but it was better than no protection.

He grabbed his Pop-Tart. "Finish eating. I need to go see if any of the ewes have lambed and bring them into the barn." He was gone, leaving her to look around and sip her orange juice.

Justin's house was cute. Square and quaint, it resembled the farmhouse look from when she'd done her online search, only it was newer construction and well-cared for. Cylindrical grain bins jutted from the snow and two silver, rounded buildings lined the end of the drive.

Dragging in a fortifying breath, she slipped outside. Aaron always left his truck running, so she abandoned it. Raising her scarf higher, she picked across the driveway to the barn Aaron had disappeared into.

A mixture of manure and pure animal hit her. Bleats greeted her, along with the low murmuring of Aaron's voice.

He backed out of a stall and saw her as she was wrinkling

her nose. "Hey. Sorry about the smell. With ewes and lambs inside, there's more…you know."

"It's not as strong as I expected." Honestly. Peejong had raised pigs when she was younger, and this was much better.

"We clean it out regularly. And the sheep are new tenants. Wanna see a newborn lamb?"

She treaded through the straw toward him.

He didn't open the gate, but there was enough space between the slats. Several bundles of white stood about by larger sheep.

"Aw, they're cute." She squatted down. A couple were sleeping with the mamas and the rest were poking around the adults as they ate.

Aaron grinned. "I know, right? We keep teasing Justin that when he wants to settle down, he needs to wait for lambing season and offer tours. There were no new lambs last night so that saves me some time and paperwork. Good thing. Justin is as anal as his brother about records. You can stay here while I feed the rest of the flock."

"I'll help." This was a whole new world, but some aspects were familiar. Peejong transitioned to farming only after her grandparents died, and she remembered parts of it. And doing this in winter added an extra layer of interest.

Aaron got the grain and supplement ready. She was assigned hay and water. But by the time she pitched all the hay she needed, he'd already scraped the troughs clean, filled them, and replenished the water.

His jacket hung open over his overalls. With the sweat gathering at the base of her hat, she might also need to ventilate.

"You do this every day?"

"Justin does with the sheep. Cash with the cattle. The rest of us fill in, until farming's back in full swing."

"They depend on you."

He was spread thin across his own family and his share of the business, but his extended family depended on him as well. Add in taking care of her and he had a lot on his plate.

No wonder he'd had to cut his trip short when he was visiting her.

She was about to ditch her hay pile when he said, "Time to feed the rest."

The rest?

The morning flew by; her stomach growled. She hadn't eaten since the Pop-Tart, and a warm lunch sounded like a trip to the spa. She liked to think she might've been a help to Aaron, but the time it had taken him to explain a task, he could've finished it himself.

He never said anything. Not when he was feeding circles around her and doing pretty much everything.

"We'll break for lunch and come back to move the older lambs and their ewes out of the lambing jug."

Yay… They were coming back.

SHE HAD MORE fun moving the lambs. Especially after they'd gone back to Aaron's and a chicken and rice mix was ready in the slow cooker—enough for everyone living under that roof.

When had he had the time to do that?

Waiting outside the barn, she wandered around. The day had warmed up to feel pleasant compared to the morning weather. At the beginning of the year, she would've shivered to death in these temperatures, but now she only wore a sweatshirt and her snowpants. Aaron disappeared to do another sweep, looking for new lambs before they left.

"All right. That's done for another two hours." He swaggered out of the barn. He'd only tugged his coveralls back on over his jeans and plaid shirt. Did his hat sit on his head straight anymore? His perpetually crooked hat was endearing, but her fingers itched to straighten it, more to take care of him than for aesthetics.

Wait, what'd he say? They were coming back *again*?

"Every two hours, you have to check for lambs?" This was supposed to be her time with him. They were together, but was it really quality time if he assigned her one part of the flock and he went in a separate direction?

It needed to be done, and Aaron did what had to be done.

He nodded. "Justin says he breaks at midnight but is back out by six. If the temperatures dip down too far, then I'm sure he checks sometime in the middle of the night." He unzipped his coveralls and dug his phone out. "Oh hey. Wanna run to town with me? Cash texted. They ran out of diapers and Abbi's not feeling well. The others are hunkered down with their babies for the day, except for Brock and Josie, but they might not have answered."

His easy grin was laced with apology.

She'd be with him, and it was better than being stuck inside four walls. "Sure. I might need to change."

"Nah. Just peel your snow pants off and grab a different coat. Voila, outfit change."

She glanced down at her muck-covered boots. It wouldn't be voila until she put on shoes without manure.

They ran back to the house and dumped their dirty clothes and headed to town.

In the store, they giggled over diapers. Partly because neither of them had any idea of what to buy. Aaron had to call Cash, and then they chuckled at the rumors it'd start when people saw her and Aaron in the baby section.

"Don't get me wrong," Aaron said. "I want kids someday. My age might be ticking away, but I'd like you to myself for a while. What about you?"

She'd like him to herself, too, but would that ever be possible? "Yes, but not now. I'd like to get settled first and get used to being married."

Heat flooded her cheeks. In a couple of weeks she'd share his last name, openly share his bed, and spring was already on its way.

Her mood started matching the weather. Bright and optimistic.

They arrived at Cash's with diapers tucked under their arms. Aaron had grabbed a pizza for the tired parents.

He didn't have the chance to knock on the door before it swung open. A tear-drop shaped bundle was cradled against Cash's shoulder, but he didn't look like the happy, first-time dad. His face was drawn and shadows hovered in his eyes.

"Good, you brought Dalisay." His smile was tight. "You went to nursing school, right?"

"Oh…I didn't finish…" Having the attention of both men turned on her was like standing alone in the spotlight. The rest of the house was quiet. Her gaze landed on the baby boy, but he seemed fine.

"Can you take a look at Abbi? She's being stubborn like a wolverine. I've been telling her to go into the doctor all day, but she refuses to"—he threw in air quotes, careful of his bundle—"'cause any trouble.' Maybe if someone with a medical background can convince her to go, or convince me I'm being a paranoid ass."

Dalisay stepped in. What was she going to be able to do? Cash pointed her to the bedroom. Leaving the two men to whisper together, she padded down the hall.

Cash and Abbi's bedroom door hung open. Dalisay knocked.

Abbi's eyelids slit open. "Dalisay, come on in. Cash sent you to talk some sense into me."

The woman was pale, and every move lacked effort.

While the rest of her skin shone like porcelain, her cheeks were flushed. Spurred by concern, Dalisay crossed into the room, her hesitation gone.

Touching her hand to Abbi's forehead, her worry deepened. "Have you taken your temperature yet?"

Abbi blinked, another move that was almost slow motion. "No. I suspected I had a fever and took something for it."

It may not have been enough. "Where's a thermometer?"

Abbi turned her head into the pillows, already falling back asleep. "Ugh, I hurt. My throat hurts, my bones hurt. I just want to sleep." She sighed and pointed to the door. "We have one for Carter. Cash can grab it."

Dalisay scurried out. "Thermometer."

Cash didn't ask any questions. He dug it out of a baby caddy and handed it over.

Back in Abbi's room, the girl didn't twitch. Her eyes stayed closed as Dalisay swiped the device across her forehead.

Abbi's breathing rate was fine, her pulse okay, but her temperature was too high, especially if she'd already taken something.

"I really think you should go in, Abbi."

Abbi frowned, squirming under covers. "I just can't get warm. It can wait until morning, right? I'll make an appointment with my own doctor."

"If you've taken fever-reducing medicine and still have a fever this high, you need to be looked at."

Abbi didn't look convinced. Her face was so washed out, the effort of getting dressed and going to the clinic was probably too daunting.

"Abbi, Cash is worried sick. I'm worried. Please go in. If it turns out to be nothing, no one gets hurt. I know you're tired, but they could help you get better."

"All right." Abbi sighed. "But I won't win any fashion awards."

Cash had the baby loaded into the carrier and passed him off to Aaron within minutes to help Abbi. Dalisay went outside with Aaron and clicked the car seat into place and helped load a tired and apologetic Abbi.

The pickup flew away. Dalisay glanced at Aaron. He beamed at her.

"What?" she asked. Self-consciousness snuck in.

"First, Mark Rio and now Abbi. I think you might have knack for this stuff."

She shrugged and walked back to their ride. "I didn't do anything special." Anyone could've done what she'd done.

"But with your cousin you jumped in before I could and managed to calm him. Abbi would've turned us all down, but she couldn't say no to you."

"It's all in the tone," she teased. "Cash would do anything she wanted, and she wanted to try to stay home."

"Very true. Still, it's a gift."

Not a gift she could do anything with.

"Why don't I ask the boys to do the lamb runs this evening and we go out to eat?"

Dalisay's smile could've cracked her face. The weariness from the early morning and the spurt of adrenaline clashed inside of her. She was tired to her bones, but in better shape than Abbi had been in. Restless energy swirled around her. She wanted to know how Abbi was doing, but like with her cousin, the event had driven home everything she'd missed out on and would still miss out on.

Slowly, she was starting to accept that nursing school wasn't in her future. But her future was here, with Aaron, with his family, jumping in where they needed her, and that she could live with.

# CHAPTER 19

One week and he'd be a married man. One week and three days.

Justin had returned and lamb duty had been turned back over. It didn't free up as much time as he'd hoped because they were heading into planting season.

And since he had a suite booked all next weekend for their wedding, he had catching up to do.

The morning dawned with a promise of sun and more melting snow. He slipped out of his temporary room and glanced at the closed door of his bedroom, the one he'd snuck out of hours ago. Soon, they'd be officially sharing it.

When Cash had called back that night and informed them that Abbi had been diagnosed with both influenza and strep throat, he'd gushed his thanks over and over for the magic Daisy had worked to convince her to go in.

The incident with Cash and Abbi had infused a new life Aaron hadn't seen in Daisy. Her smile came quicker, but the cloud of sorrow at her missed career still hung over her. They'd find a way. Once she got her driver's license, she'd see that commuting wasn't impossible. If he had to drive her, they'd make it work.

If it took years, and they had kids, he'd rock and bottle and strap the kid on to make Daisy's dreams come true.

He was filling his orange juice when Daisy's voice drifted down the hall. The door was shut, but she was talking fast. He didn't recognize any words. Was she speaking to her mother?

It didn't sound like it. Her speech was clipped. Frantic?

He abandoned his glass and drifted down the hall. Daisy wasn't bothering to smother her volume. Was everything all right?

The door flew open, the light blinding him. He blinked as Daisy charged right into his chest.

"Whoa. Everything okay?"

She held the phone to her chest, her face tight. "Ina fell. She broke both her wrists. Her employers have taken her to the hospital. She's going into surgery."

He enclosed her in his arms. She sought solace for a second, but then spun out of his embrace.

"She won't be able to work. Her employers didn't say, but they can't hold her position. She'll need months to recover." She stumbled into the bedroom and stared at her suitcase. "She won't have a place to stay. I have to take care of her."

"What about the rest of the family?"

A choked sob came from Daisy. She pressed her hand against her head, her gaze still on her luggage. "Sally will help care for her, as much as Ina will detest being helpless around her." Daisy's hand dropped. She turned on him, her eyes watery. "Then what? Her injuries are so bad they need surgery. She'll be dependent on someone for months."

A slow realization dawned on him. Daisy hadn't said it yet, but she wanted to go home. Anyone in her position would. And she should be able to.

Only… They weren't married yet. Leaving would nullify her visa. His throat constricted.

"Daisy."

Her eyes were stricken, her face pale. She was hurting. "I need to go back," she said in a ragged whisper.

He nodded. Because talking might make him do something like cry, and he wasn't ready for the reality to set in.

"It's, uh… almost seven in the morning. We could wait until the courthouse opens."

Daisy sniffled and looked away. "She's going into surgery. I'm not sure how long it'll take, but I need to start back as soon as possible."

*As soon as possible.* But if she nullified the visa, they'd have to reapply again, and it'd be months before he could see her.

"Only a few more hours and we could get married before you go." He stepped toward her, but she jerked into action. She lifted her case onto the bed, then went to the dresser to pack her things.

His heart strummed a hard beat. She needed to leave. They weren't married yet, and they'd be an ocean apart. Then what?

"I want you to be with your mom, Daisy. I'll do everything I can to make it happen."

She still didn't look at him, but her shoulders shook as she dragged clothing off the hangers in the closet.

"But, what about us?" He could go visit her, but spring was here. Planting season. Long hours in the field. Longer hours away.

Tears streamed from her dark eyes. "It wouldn't be fair to you. You wanted to celebrate the day with your family." She dumped her armload into the suitcase. Her hands landed on her hips. "How am I going to buy a ticket?"

Her strangled voice kicked him into action. She was hurting. Worry for her mother was paramount, but like him, the question of them was killing her.

What about them?

He dug out his wallet and laid his credit card on the covers of the bed. After they were married, they were going to open a joint account. He'd been looking forward to when he could introduce Daisy Walker around town.

The dream was fading.

He caught her by the shoulders. "Look. You get home. Take care of Mari. You and I will figure it out."

She caught her bottom lip between white teeth. Was she stopping herself from disagreeing?

They'd be okay.

To prove his confidence in them crossing this hurdle, he picked his card back up. "You finish packing. *I'll* reserve your tickets."

She peered at him for a moment. "You take care of everyone, Aaron. Thank you."

Why'd that sound like a bad thing?

He left her, his feet as heavy as mason blocks, to hop on his computer. The ease of finding times that worked was bittersweet.

Daisy's voice drifted down the hall. She was on the phone again. Peejong? It had to be killing her not to know the details on Mari.

He rubbed his face and clicked through buying the rest of her tickets. If they left soon, she'd make it in plenty of time for the first flight out of town.

Picturing the mighty Mari down and frail wasn't easy. She'd been a determined ball of energy, her keen gaze always assessing him and Daisy. Both wrists. The pain the poor woman must be in.

He was being selfish with his questions about him and

Daisy. Getting her back to her mother took priority. They'd work them out later.

She hauled the bag down the hall past his office while still on the phone. A long-sleeved shirt and leggings was all she wore. He followed after her to the mudroom, where she stepped into her Chucks and left the rest of her outerwear hanging. Packing snow gear wouldn't make sense.

His gaze drifted to her snow pants and parka as they walked out the door. They'd probably hang there as reminders until she got back.

DALISAY'S STOMACH churned as she hung up with Peejong. Her brain spun over what was happening. Ina. Flying back to the Philippines. Alone. Goodbye visa and goodbye Aaron.

Anxiety over Ina's status made her nauseous. It was one thing to be in the viewpoint of the medical professional, but to be the family of a patient was a subtle form of hell. And to be thousands of miles away…the helplessness…

Both wrists. Ina would need assistance going to the bathroom and cleaning herself. Feeding herself. She'd need help dressing. She'd probably lose her job. Her employers were nice enough, but Ina had gotten hurt out in the market when she'd slipped during some bad rains. They had no responsibility otherwise. Ina had only worked for them for a few months. As much as they liked her, it was business.

Peejong and Sally were rushing to the hospital. They'd take Ina to their home after she was discharged. Daisy was welcome to stay as long as she needed. They'd figure the rest out later.

Just what Aaron had said.

Only she'd already figured it out. Before the dreadful phone call, she'd seen how much those closest to Aaron relied on him. She fully understood why he'd left the Philippines early. There was so much responsibility on his plate, and his home was here.

Sure, they could reapply for the visa, wait longer, but what about Ina? Would she recover and be able to work again? Ina needed her more than ever.

Dalisay's stomach sank. She wouldn't be able to come back to America for months. Aaron couldn't come to see her.

If they were married, she'd move heaven and earth to make him happy. But in a stasis, with her in another country, she couldn't make him happy. He wanted a marriage. Kids. To wake up to his wife each day.

They approached the airport. She rubbed her hands up and down her thighs. She wanted to scream, *No, not yet.* But she also wanted to run right onto the tarmac and crawl into the plane and demand, *Fly now.*

Without more than a few words to each other, he parked. She got out, and he grabbed her bag.

The check-in process was smooth. Only five other people milled around the tiny building. This airport had one flight going out in the morning and one in the afternoon. Good thing Ina's employer had called early enough.

They sat by each other in the waiting area. Dalisay hardly noticed the speculative looks shot their direction.

Did they know Aaron? Did they think she was leaving him?

They'd be right.

She checked her phone every few minutes. No calls. No updates. Until Peejong reached the hospital, there wouldn't be any. By the time surgery was over, she'd be en route and the doctor might not be able to get through.

She released a shaky breath and stared at the ceiling. Aaron rubbed circles between her shoulder blades. Having his support meant everything.

Losing his support darkened her world.

"Aaron—"

The announcement for the flight blared with static from the lone speaker in the room.

"Time to go." He stood and held out his hand.

She accepted his touch one last time. Tears sprang into her eyes. "I'm afraid this is the end."

"We'll work it out."

She shook her head, her hair a heavy mantle offering little comfort. "No, Aaron. I'm sorry, but this has to be it between us."

Color drained from his face. "What?"

The other passengers filed out the exit. She'd chosen the coward's way. They could've talked all the way here, but the pain ripped her apart and made her head spin.

"You have so many people here. I can't come back—"

"Of course, you can. I'll re-file when I get home—"

She squeezed his coat. "And then what? I wait for six months? Can you come out and see me?"

He opened his mouth, but his words faltered.

"Exactly. You want someone who'll be around. Someone who'll be a help, not a hindrance. I can't be that person. This emergency has showed me that."

"But, Daisy." He caressed her cheek, his voice a whisper. "I love you. We can make this work."

She squeezed her eyes shut. It was the first time he'd said those words. She'd felt them for so long, but neither of them had ventured there. Had that been a sign they knew the plan was going to implode?

"How can we?" She sounded like she was begging.

"I'll just... We can..."

"See? We don't even know where to start." Her hot tears streaked over his fingers on her face. "I love you, too. So much." She steeled herself and went for the heart of the matter. "You had a hard time getting away for two weeks. I was trying to get away from an isolated existence that offered me nothing, but that's…"

His features tightened. It was dawning on him, too.

He could've made her happy, brightened each day, but would that have helped make his house any less of a prison?

She stood on her tiptoes and planted a hasty kiss on his mouth. He didn't twitch, just watched her with abject disbelief.

Sniffling, she grabbed her ticket. "You need to let me go. It'll be easier this way."

His hand dropped from her. "I don't want to. I want to keep fighting."

"It would be a waste of time. Each mile between us would win. Goodbye, Aaron."

She kept her head down as she approached the ticket agent.

"Thank you," the older woman said, her voice low, like an apology. She handed the ticket back and gave Dalisay's hand a squeeze. "Go on in, sweetie. I'll make sure he's okay."

Coughing through a sob, Dalisay scurried to the plane.

Her heart shattered into more pieces with each step, but she forced herself to be strong. She could collapse in her seat. And face her regrets while she sat alone on the flight home.

# CHAPTER 20

*A*aron dumped his lunch into the tractor and backed out. He hit his head on the doorframe but didn't bother swearing. He was used to pain.

Daisy wouldn't return his calls. She only answered his texts, saying Ina was out of surgery and it'd be a long recovery. Then she'd asked him to quit contacting her.

So he did. And he regretted it every day.

Maybe he could wear her down.

But she'd been right. He couldn't leave his job, his brothers, his parents, or his cousins that had marriages and kids of their own to take care of.

She'd alluded to being miserable here. He was confident that once winter was over and they were married that would've changed. But she'd still be without the career she wanted because of him, while supporting him in his profession of choice.

It wasn't fair to her. She'd said it wouldn't be fair to him, but a life without her wasn't the key to happiness.

But he had fields to plant. Then he had fields to spray. Then he had fields to harvest. Then it'd be winter and

Nicolas would be in his senior year, and there were would be cattle and sheep to help with.

The same thoughts plagued him every day. He wanted to tear his head off and dropkick it across the shop. Missing her was killing him.

Two weeks, and the agony was as fresh as when she'd cut his heart out in the airport.

The ticket agent, Mrs. Downs, had consoled him when he'd dropped into the chair after Daisy left. He hardly knew her, but her husband had farmed and was an acquaintance. Mrs. Downs had been his only hold on sanity while the plane took off.

The weekend he was supposed to get married had passed. He'd gotten shit-faced at Lucas's house. Two pathetic, single fucks lamenting over the women who left them. Good thing no one had told them when they were fifteen that this was their future.

Aaron had thrown himself into his work since then. Which meant his days hadn't changed and how sad was that?

His phone rang. Well, there was something new. His family, all of them, had maintained radio silence. They'd left him to grieve the loss of his fiancée.

He checked the screen. It was Dillon. Had the eldest cousin decreed his mourning period over?

"What?" Aaron snapped into the phone. That may be another reason they'd backed off. He was a moody bastard and didn't care.

"Can you come into the house? I need to talk to you."

"About what?"

But Dillon had disconnected.

Fucker.

Aaron stomped across the gravel to the house. The birds sang, too damn cheerful for an early April day. Tulips peeked out of the dirt in his flowerbeds. The ones he'd prepared to gussy up for Daisy.

There was one task he didn't have to do anymore.

Dillon's truck was parked in front of his house. Why couldn't he come to the shop?

Aaron stormed inside and kicked his boots off. The mudroom was a damn mess. But, hey, Daisy's winter gear was gone. Mom moved off her ass to do that.

Or maybe it was Jackson. He was a perceptive kid when he needed to be.

Aaron rounded the corner. Dillon was the first person he saw. A sense of déjà vu hit him. Cash, Travis, and Brock were also there. His brothers were on the couch, watching him. Where were their ever-present phones?

"Is this an intervention?" Because what could they do? Tell him to get over the love of his life?

Not gonna happen.

"Sort of," Dad said. "Dillon and I have been talking…"

Awesome.

Dillon filled in. "It seems that from your story of Dalisay leaving, you feel like you can't go and be with her."

Aaron's eyes widened. His expression had to say *you've got to be fucking kidding me.* "Uh, no. I have a job." He swept his arm out, frustration and anger fueling words he'd probably regret. "Mom sure isn't raising the boys. Someone's got to. Someone has to be the backup so you all can live your tidy little lives."

Since he was the last one to settle down and still couldn't find someone to tolerate his apparently shitty existence.

A sharp inhale from Mom spurred a thread of guilt. He quashed it. Someone had to say it.

"Your father and I have been talking…" Mom said.

Was this going to turn out as fabulous as Dillon and Dad discussing his life?

She brushed her hair out of her face and clasped her hands on her lap. What she was going to say bothered her. "I…need to go back on my depression meds."

"Depression?" He'd never heard her speak of suffering from depression.

She nodded. "I don't like to talk about it, but after the boys were born, I started having problems. I'd been off them for a while before we sold the farm and house, but"—she glanced at Dad—"I think the change unbalanced everything."

Aaron swallowed past a lump in his throat. "I'm sorry, I didn't know."

"I know you're going to want to blame yourself, but this has nothing to do with you, Aaron." Her tone was firm, so much like the mom he knew.

Dad adjusted his hat. "What we're trying to say is that you need to go and be with Dalisay and we'll take care of everything."

Aaron stared at him. It was like someone holding a piece of carrot cake in front of him after he'd been fasting for a month. So promising, but in reality, it'd make him sick. Dad could make all the offers he wanted, but backing them up was the only part that counted.

And more guilt haunted Aaron. "But you're retired. You shouldn't have to dive back into a full planting season when you're supposed to be enjoying your days."

Dad's expression turned troubled and he glanced at Dillon. Dillon nodded.

What had those two talked about?

"I wasn't ready to retire when we sold the farm. But Dillon's dad was sick, and it was such a solid plan, a good one to get you boys started." Dad lifted a shoulder. "I gave in. I didn't expect…to not know how to do anything else but farm."

All the times Dad had offered to help him ran through

Aaron's head. Aaron had thought he'd been the one helping Dad out, but he'd only been adding more work to his plate and adding to Dad's misery.

Jackson cleared his throat. "Nicolas and I can help out more. I'll be home all summer."

"And I'll be around all next year," Nicolas said.

Aaron looked to each of his cousins. Did he dare get his hopes up?

Cash spoke. "You'd do this for all of us. We can do it for you."

"But getting Dalisay back could take months." He could at least fly out and see her. It wouldn't be enough, but he could plead his case.

"Then stay for months," Brock said.

Aaron gazed at all of them. Stay for months. Months. It couldn't be possible. "She doesn't even want me to call her anymore."

"She's gotta be having the same regrets," Travis said. "It was clear how crazy she was over you. You two have been together for what, six months? And you broke it off and cancelled the wedding in like two minutes. Go get closure at the very least."

Dillon nodded. "But if she sees that you're able to leave the farm, she might not feel like marrying you is a prison sentence. No offense."

Aaron dropped his gaze. His cousins sympathized with her. How awful would it be for her to spend her life with him?

"Dude, I can see your brain working," Cash said. "You work too much. That's all. We're not saying she has to be convinced that life with you out here wouldn't be hell frozen over." He grinned. "Well, six months out of the year it is, but we'll get her a four-wheel drive."

Aaron shoved his hands in his pockets. "So I go over

there. I win her back and she moves here. Then what? I'll still farm. I'll still be me."

Cash shrugged. "Then you'll have to learn how to say no and ask for help. And we'll watch out for you."

Mom wrung her hands together. "And we'll move out."

Aaron shook his head. "No. You two are happier out here. I don't think your presence is a deal breaker."

It'd be easier for Dad to help if he lived out here, too.

"Well, talk to her first," Mom said. "If we're an issue, we'll move. We don't want to get in the way of your happiness."

Aaron nodded. With their support he could do it. He should've done it without their support. Another trip to the Philippines. Should he call first?

Seriously. Was he thinking about doing this?

Yes. He missed the morning flight out, but it wasn't too late for the afternoon one. Or his cousins could live up to their promise to help and drive him to the cities to catch a flight.

The groundwork for the plan had been laid by his family. The rest bloomed in his mind. He'd fly to Solano, seek out Peejong, and track Daisy down from there.

"Ina! Let me do that." Dalisay rushed into the comfort room at Peejong's.

"I can stand up on my own," Ina huffed.

"Yes, but if you fall again you won't be able to get yourself back up." Dalisay yanked up Ina's pants.

"Is Sally here?" Ina muttered.

"No, she ran to Solano with the boys. Peejong has a load to sell at the market."

Relief flitted across Ina's face. Both of her arms were in casts. Her left wrist was a clean break and in a normal cast.

Her right wrist, which was her dominant hand, had required surgery with pins and screws. They had another checkup in Solano next week, but for now, Ina was supposed to rest.

Dalisay suppressed a sigh. If only Ina was back on the pain meds, she might rest. Instead, Dalisay ran after her as Ina tried to be useful. One trip and fall, and her mother would face-plant and be unable to get herself up. She could rebreak her bones or bust some new ones.

"Then I'll take a walk." Ina shook her hips to adjust her clothing as much as she could. "I don't need her running after me with another lecture." She strode out of the bathroom, her back straight and her head high.

Dalisay pushed her hair off her face and treaded after her. Ina looked more put together than she did. Taking care of her mother would be nothing, but Aunt Sally kept her running ragged. They didn't pay rent, but Dalisay was paying in sweat.

Peejong had asked her about Michael the other day. Barely two weeks since she'd broken off her engagement—as Peejong pointed out, her second engagement. Aunt Sally had chided Peejong, but the delay wouldn't last long. They wanted to see her married and happy and have her close by because as much as they frustrated her, they loved her. And she loved them.

And she'd missed them.

Not as much as—

She doubled down her attention on her mother. Thinking of Aaron would only encourage more crying. She saved that for the dead of night when everyone was sleeping. In the tiny room she shared with Ina, she could turn her back to the world and let the tears flow.

Ina chose her footsteps carefully. Her gait was slow. She tired easily, but it was so soon after the injury. Her walks weren't long or far, but they dulled her restless edge.

"You have not heard from him lately?" Ina asked.

Dalisay's world dimmed despite the full sun. She'd told Ina the story, then had repeated it when Ina's thoughts were clearer. Beyond that, Ina hadn't pried.

"I asked him to quit contacting me." It was too hard.

"If I had not fallen, you would be married by now." Matter-of-fact. But Ina's guilt was there.

"Your emergency only highlighted major issues between us."

"But you two would have worked through them."

"At what cost? How often would I have gotten to fly back and see you? And…what would I have done with my life?"

"Have kids?"

Dalisay also didn't miss the hopefulness in Ina's voice. "We both wanted them, but I…"

"Wanted more than motherhood." Now that was said like she knew how it felt.

"Yes. I was only with him for two months, but it was the longest time of my life, Ina. I loved spending every second with him, but when he wasn't around, and it was often, there was nothing for me. Is that selfish?"

"I'm too young to think so." Ina smiled. Her eyes twinkled with mirth, the first sign that Ina's spirit hadn't been destroyed. "I was just like you when I married your father. Only my parents weren't. They were very old-fashioned."

Dalisay wanted to give Ina a giant hug, but it'd hurt her arms. "It wasn't that he forced me to be that way, it just was. Maybe we could've changed it, but when I had to leave before getting married, it showed me… He's married to the farm more than he'd be married to me." The dam burst, and all her thoughts and concerns spilled out. The complete relief of being able to talk to her mom—in person—fueled her. "Do I want to take every flight home alone because he can't leave Moore? Do I want to go years in between seeing you and

Peejong?" She swept her hand toward the house. "What about the boys? Living in Manila, I got to still see them once or twice a year. In Moore, it'd all be online."

"And Aaron's family? Don't you feel the same about them?"

Dalisay shrugged. Did she? "Maybe a little. Jackson's graduating this year. Ina, he's so smart and considerate. I think Nicolas is more like Aaron was when he was younger. And Jackson has this big dance coming up. He showed me his date's dress. It's gorgeous—"

She frowned. Had she grown closer to the Walkers than she thought?

Had she been too wrapped up in her insecurities to see how comfortable she was there?

Ina huffed out a breath. "My back is getting sore. I need to return."

They shuffled back. Before the house came into view between the palm trees, an engine rattled in the distance.

Ina sucked on her teeth. "Is that them already? I was hoping for more sanity time."

Dalisay giggled. "It's not bad here. We get our own room."

Ina quirked a brow. "Not bad for visiting. But do you want to room with me for the rest of my life?"

"It won't be so bad when we're out in the field all day," Dalisay joked.

Ina snorted. If they could make light of their situation like this it wouldn't be bad, for long.

Ina grew serious. "Why'd you really break up with him? Why not wait and reapply for the visa?"

Dalisay had given Ina several reasons why. They all seemed reasonable. But like Ina had noticed, none of them were true barriers. Obstacles, yes. Insurmountable? No.

"He's worked so hard for everyone else, was it really fair to make him wait months to years longer? I want a career. He wants kids. I want kids, too, but I'm only twenty-three. He's almost thirty."

His birthday was at the end of May. How would he celebrate? Would he finally meet someone? Melancholy settled over her. She'd have to find a way to keep her mind busy that day.

"Add to all that the extra time to get me back to the States, and it wasn't fair to him."

Ina nodded. Not in the way that said *I absolutely agree with you*, but slower, like she could see where Dalisay was coming from, but didn't agree.

The rectangular house came into view. All was quiet. Perhaps Peejong had to drop supplies and head back out. He was being so generous. She should feel guilty for not wanting him around. The solitude was a balm for her at times. Other times, it was a special form of torture.

"You think I made a mistake," Dalisay said as they rounded the path.

"I don't know that there's any right or wrong in this situation."

Dalisay glanced at Ina's stoic features. "But?"

"They say, 'follow your heart.' Except, in this case, I think your heart looked to your head for a reason why it was hurting, and you interpreted it as a failure in the relationship."

"I don't know, Ina. It's too late, regardless. He's quit calling." *Because I asked him to.*

Ina sucked in a breath. Dalisay glanced up and stopped, her hand flying to her chest. Her heart thudded once, twice. Ina looked at her, then back at the house, her eyes wide.

Aaron stood in the doorway. He'd been squinting around the yard, as if wondering where everyone was at. But when he met Dalisay's gaze, he took his cap off and clenched it in his fists. His hair remained flattened, like he hadn't removed the cap for days, but with the April heat kicking up, hat head could happen within minutes.

Why was she noticing something so silly? Her dream man stood on her doorstep.

"Aaron?" Duh. Of course it was him. But why was he here?

Did she care? She tore away from Ina and sprinted toward Aaron. He was here! In a remote farm in the Philippines, thousands of miles away from home.

She refused to believe he'd flown all the way here to get the last word in.

Her only fear as she flew toward him was that he was a hallucination, that she missed him so hard her mind conjured his image.

Real or not, he opened his arms for her. A strangled sound left her throat as she plowed into him.

Strong arms closed around her in an all-too-familiar embrace. She smashed her face against his chest and cried. "I'm so sorry."

"My flower." His hold tightened, his head resting on top of hers. "There's nothing to be sorry about. I have a lot of apologizing to do."

She pulled back. His shirt was already covered in drops of wetness from her tears. "Why? I was impulsive and irrational."

His small smile crinkled his eyes. He peeled his gaze off her as if it was the last thing he wanted to do, but when he saw Ina, his brows popped. "How are you doing?"

As he crossed to Ina, Dalisay got tucked into his side. This. It was like his body was made to shelter her.

Ina waved him off and switched to English for him. "Fine. You two talk. I must nap."

"I'll help," Dalisay said.

"Pssht. I can lay myself down." Ina's stern gaze oscillated

between the two of them. Before she passed them, she stopped. "Are you staying for a while?"

Aaron's expression turned solemn. "As long as I need to."

Dalisay's heart jumped. He hadn't lasted a week last time and like he'd said, it was his busy season. "But how…? The farm?"

His grin was easy and slightly abashed. "Turns out, Dad never wanted to retire, so he doesn't mind taking over, even if it means months. I hope it means months."

His dad might back out? Wait, Aaron was looking to her for confirmation.

Dalisay caught her slack jaw. "You're going to stay here for months?"

Ina's attention was as riveted as hers. The nap must not have been urgent.

"I'll stay as long as I need to if you still want to marry me. If you still want to move to America, to a small town, with a farmer." He swallowed. "But I understand if you want to stay here. Then I'll beg to stay with you. Because, Daisy, I love you too much to give up."

Her breath caught. "But I gave up."

"No." He stepped closer and brushed her cheek with the backs of his fingers. "You showed me how selfish I was being. You were making a huge sacrifice and I was coasting along like I always do. The guys—my cousins—said they'll make sure I start asking for help and quit working so much. And they'll get you a four-wheel drive vehicle."

Her eyes drifted shut as she leaned into his touch. The memories haunted her dreams. "You're anything but selfish. I love you, Aaron. And if you're staying here, I think we have plenty of time to plan how we're going to make this work."

His grin stole the air from her lungs. He dropped to one knee, not making a sound on the spongy ground, and presented her with the ring she'd returned. "Dalisay Calamba

Cortez, will you do me the honor of marrying me here, in front of all your family, then again in front of all of mine?"

Her hands flew to her mouth. It was the perfect proposal, on so many levels. It was Aaron. He still wanted to marry her. She'd get to celebrate with her relatives—and Ina. And he'd share the moment again with his relatives.

This man was far from selfish. His generosity was a trait that only made her love him more, and she'd spend the rest of her life proving that to him.

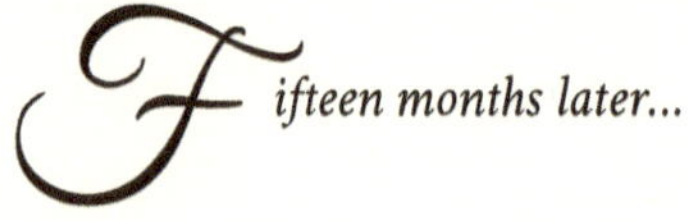

*ifteen months later…*

DALISAY GRINNED at Aaron as he handed her a container with a sandwich and apple slices, and a water bottle. She slid them into her backpack and shouldered it.

"I'm about to burst with pride," he said. His blue eyes twinkled, and he didn't quit smiling.

So she wasn't alone. It'd been a long road, but here they were at their house in Moore. She was going to her first day of paramedic school. After a lot of research and soul-searching, the decision had been surprisingly easy. Maybe nursing school was still in her future, but the excitement of field medicine couldn't be ignored, neither could the convenience of the location of the program at MCC.

Aaron walked her out of the house. They'd been back in America for almost nine months. After they'd arrived, they'd filed the paperwork for moving Ina over. She had arrived a few months after them and lived in the spare room Aaron had used before they were married.

Aaron's parents still lived in the basement. Dalisay liked having them around, especially since Lori had made huge gains in her mental health. She smiled easier, and she even emerged from the basement every day. A year ago, she'd started her own small interior design business, growing it slowly. *It's more of a hobby*, she'd say, but Dalisay thought it was an important step in her treatment.

Dalisay's first summer in Moore had only cemented her growing love and dedication to her new home. When the fields ripened, and the ditches and trees were green and blooming, it was breathtaking—and warm. Still, there was a special serenity in winter that she enjoyed while it was there.

Aaron had dived back into work, but not until after their wedding reception, and not like before. His dad split his time between helping Aaron and doing the part-time farmhand work for Lucas.

She and Aaron had crossed some formidable hurdles to get to this point, but they'd done it together. Peejong and Sally had kept them both busy, but Aaron had said it was pure enjoyment—all the fun of farming with none of the responsibility.

And the guy Peejong had tried setting her up with had gotten married and had a kid on the way by the time she and Aaron flew to the States.

Aaron opened the door to her new SUV, a hybrid but with four-wheel drive. She deposited her items inside, her belly flipping at the task of walking into a new school.

"Nervous," Aaron asked, attuned to her.

"A little. First day jitters."

Ina hurried out the door. "Oh good. I didn't miss you." She wrapped Dalisay in a big embrace. "He gave you the lunch I packed, right?"

Dalisay chuckled. Ina was healed, with only a few remaining aches. She refused to sit still, and the house had never looked better. Between her cleaning and Lori's talents, the place was updated and homey. Meals continued to be rotated among all of them under the same roof, but with the boys in college, Dalisay ended up cooking at least once a week and Ina picked up the extras.

"I'm gonna be in the field all day," Aaron said. "But I'll be back to hear how your day went."

"It's harvest season. You don't have to."

He smiled. "I can work late every other day. This one is special." He glanced at Ina. "We're sending our girl to school."

Dalisay gave her another quick hug. Ina scurried inside. The kiss from Aaron reminded her why she didn't get a full night of sleep.

Worth it.

She hopped into her vehicle and pulled away. As she neared the end of the drive, Kami passed on the main road. She honked and waved.

Aaron's relatives surrounded her, and she wouldn't have it any other way. She missed her extended family, but having Ina around meant more than the world to her. And they planned to fly back every winter during her school breaks.

When they had kids in a few years, their trips might dwindle, but Peejong had mentioned flying everyone out to visit once in a while. He was probably more interested in seeing Aaron's farm than in seeing America. The two had grown close during Aaron's time in Solano. The relationship seemed to take the edge off Sally's interference in her life.

That bleak day in the airport when she thought she lost Aaron forever had ripped her apart. Her world had ended, and she'd only planned to exist and help her mother.

But now? Not only did she have Aaron, but she was

surrounded by love and support. Life was richer than she'd ever imagined.

----------------

Get more of Moore in the spin-off series Part-Time Cowboys. Book one, Rancher in Training, kicks off with Jesse from the first book in this series.

For all the latest news, sneak peeks, quarterly short stories, and free material sign up for my newsletter.

Thank you for reading. I'd love to know what you thought. Please consider leaving a review for Mail Order Farmer at the retailer the book was purchased from.
~Marie

# ABOUT THE AUTHOR

Marie Johnston writes paranormal and contemporary romance. Before she was a writer, she was a microbiologist. Depending on the situation, she can be oddly unconcerned about germs or weirdly phobic. She's also a licensed medical technician and has worked as a public health microbiologist and as a lab tech in hospital and clinic labs. Marie's been a volunteer EMT, a college instructor, a security guard, a phlebotomist, a hotel clerk, and a coffee pourer in a bingo hall. All fodder for a writer!! She has four kids, an old cat, and a puppy that's bigger than half her kids.

mariejohnstonwriter.com
Facebook
Twitter @mjohnstonwriter